SONNY'S HOUSE OF SPIES

Other Novels by George Ella Lyon

Borrowed Children

The Stranger I Left Behind

Here and Then

With a Hammer for My Heart

Gina.Jamie.Father.Bear.

SONNY'S HOUSE OF SPIES

George Ella Lyon

A Richard Jackson Book
Atheneum Books for Young Readers
New York   London   Toronto   Sydney

For Leatha Kendrick,
whose friendship nurtures all my words

Atheneum Books for Young Readers
An imprint of Simon & Schuster
Children's Publishing Division
1230 Avenue of the Americas
New York, New York 10020

Book design by Ann Sullivan
The text of this book is set in Trade Gothic.

Printed in the United States of America
First Edition
10 9 8 7 6 5 4 3 2 1

Library of Congress Cataloging-in-Publication Data
Lyon, George Ella, 1949–
Sonny's house of spies / George Ella Lyon.— 1st ed.
p. cm.
"A Richard Jackson Book."
Summary: In a small Alabama town in 1947–1956, Sonny searches for answers about his father's disappearance, "Uncle Marty," who looks after the family, and Mamby, their black housekeeper.
ISBN 0-689-85168-5
[1. Coming of age—Fiction. 2. Family problems—Fiction.
3. Single-parent families—Fiction. 4. Race relations—Fiction.
5. Homosexuality—Fiction. 6. Alabama—History—20th century—Fiction.] I. Title.
PZ7.L9954So 2004
[Fic]—dc21
2003007529

✸

Without Dick Jackson's prompting, I would never have heard Sonny's voice. Without Kendra Marcus' belief that there was something larger in it, I would never have found the whole story. My deep thanks to both of them.

Thanks also to my family, my Word Sisters, and to Greg Higgins, owner and baker at Magee's Bakery, who answered a hundred questions while making doughnuts at daybreak.

Part One

1947

one

You don't know my daddy.

He's strong.

He used to hold me over his head in one hand.

Now he can hold me in both hands and fly me through the air. I'm a Spitfire.

At Grandpa's he lets me stand on his shoulders and pick the highest peach off the tree.

Daddy makes things work, inside and out. He fixes the clock. He fixes the car.

And he is smart. That's what my mama is always saying: "Leon has the quickest mind of anybody."

For his work, he looks at land for the paper mill. He puts numbers on paper and draws lines with special tools and then they know how to make a road.

When we were going to Uncle Hickman's house, and I was in the backseat with my sister Loretta and Mama was up front with Daddy and the baby (who doesn't know anything, only spits and cries), Daddy said, "Sonny, someday when I'm long gone and you're driving out to the homeplace, you'll remember that your daddy built this road."

"Yes sir," I said. Long gone? Where would Daddy go?

"He means *dead*," Loretta said, pressing her thumb into my forehead so hard I was sure she'd left a dent.

I remember what Daddy said about the road.

Like I remember how he smells: tangy from shaving in the morning, sweaty and dusty at night.

But when they say, "Sonny, you just forget that," I don't remember anything.

I am good at forgetting and remembering. Mama scratched me once, real bad down my back, and I don't remember that. How she shrieked, "Now for the love of God, would you hush?"

I remember how Mamby put Mercurochrome on the scratches, how it stung and I didn't cry, and when I told her it was the neighbor's cat Zooko who scratched me 'cause he thought I was a tree, she said, "Some cat."

I don't remember when Daddy was gone for a long time and Mama said it was for business, but Grandpa said, "The road to Hell has got a layover at Natchez."

Nobody has told me to forget last night yet. Daddy

didn't come home for dinner. Mama gave us some sugar bread and put lids on all the pots on the stove. Finally it was so late that she put the baby to bed and the street-lights came on and we sat at the kitchen table and started passing bowls around. Loretta asked why we hadn't had a blessing.

Mama looked sharp at her and said, "I guess I'm not feeling very thankful."

When Loretta took her first bite, she said, "I can see why." The food had got thick and sad.

"That remark earns you the dishes," Mama told her. Loretta's only nine but she's tall. She can reach the faucets.

"I'll help," I said, hoping to stop a fight.

"Thank you, Mr. Butterfingers," Loretta said.

"He can scrape out the pots," Mama said.

Before I did that, Mama fixed another plate.

"Is that for Daddy?" Loretta asked.

Mama nodded.

That made me feel better. Daddy would be home to eat. I started scraping the yellow and green food globs into the garbage.

"Won't it get cold?" Loretta asked.

"It's already cold," Mama said. She got out a long box and unrolled foil from it to cover the plate. Then she set Daddy's dinner with its silver blanket in the oven. "I'm going to check on the baby. Sonny, you finish that and get ready for bed."

When she was out of the kitchen Loretta said, "She'll send me to bed too. We never get to see the good stuff."

I stood still, trying to think what she meant.

Loretta whapped me on the chest with a dish towel. "Stop thinking, Sonny! You'll have a spell!"

So I put the last plate on the counter and went upstairs and got into my new summer pj's with the white sailboats painted on them. I'd already had a bath back when we were hoping to eat with Daddy. I sat on my pillow with my knees up to my chin, then slid myself between the sheets like you put your hand in your pocket. That way nothing can snatch me in the night.

The phone ringing woke me up.

And Mama's voice. "We're just fine, Roo." Oh, it was Aunt Roo. That was good. "Well, no, he's not, but that doesn't mean—" She was quiet for a minute, listening. "Tell her I said she's a liar, then. A filthy liar! And you of all people shouldn't listen to her." Mama slammed down the phone.

My mama doesn't say "liar" or "filthy."

I slid out of the bed-pocket to sit on the stairs, in the shadows where she couldn't see me. I had to see if it really was my mama who said those words. But she had left the wide hall where the phone sits on the marbletop table and gone through the dark dining room to the kitchen. I heard a cupboard door open and then the rattle of dishes and she came back with Daddy's supper on a tray. She balanced this by the phone. Then she took off her shoes. My mama doesn't go barefooted. Even if she has on her nightclothes, she wears slippers.

I got sleepy, but the *uuff* of the front door woke me. It sticks a little. Then Daddy said in his saved-for-night voice, "Why, Selma!" and Mama lifted that tray to her shoulder like a waitress and heaved it at him.

"You missed your dinner, but it didn't miss you," Mama said.

I am really going to have to forget the *crash* and *splush* and *clack* of that china and silver, that roast beef and creamed corn and that little tray with the butterflies on it, and Daddy yelling, "God damn it!"

And Mama saying, "You think I don't know you're up to no good? This is humiliating, Leon. Even Roo's neighbor knew you weren't home. Why you want to throw away your plateful in this life I do not know."

But *you* threw it, Mama, I wanted to say. Why didn't you go to bed like you told us to? Why didn't you just forget it?

Daddy bent over the mess and got a glob of corn on his finger. Then he came up to Mama and wiped it on her cheek. "Because I don't like the food," he said.

And she slapped him across the face. It sounded like little thunder, and I let go my breath and the pee I'd been holding. I couldn't run to the toilet because they'd hear me. I just let it happen, like everything else. There must have been a dipperful.

Then together they picked up the broken dishes, put them on the tray, and went out to the kitchen. Later Daddy came back with a rag.

I knew then to run get in bed, because in a minute they'd be coming up the stairs.

Nobody woke me up today. Just too much light.

No smell of breakfast, no baby crying.

From the top of the stairs I saw suitcases in the hall. The front door was open.

I ran down and out, summer grass licking my feet.

Daddy was loading the car. I jumped on his back and he almost lost his balance.

"Hey, Son!" he said.

I didn't answer. I could feel sweat through the white shirt I'd watched Mamby iron yesterday. He straightened up. "No time to play monkey," he said.

I didn't move. His backbone was knobby against my cheek. His suspender so close to my eye looked like a road.

"I said, Get *down*, Sonny."

I did, but I held his arm as I slid and then I bit him on the meaty part of his hand.

"Why, you little hellion!" he said, slinging me off.

I ran into the house to get my clothes on.

My daddy's hand tasted like metal, but sweet, too, like dough, and salty like tears in a pillow slip. It tasted like clothes and the leather suitcase handle.

I got back outside as fast as I could and stood on the running board. Maybe I could hide in the car when he wasn't looking.

"Where are you going?" I asked.

"Natchez," he said.

"For how long?"

"I don't know, Sonny. It's business."

"But Grandpa says—"

"Forget what that old man says. You listen to me."

He was talking about Mama's daddy. It made me shiver. And the shivers sent Mama's words right out of my mouth: "You think I don't know—" But I *didn't* know, so I had to stop.

"Don't know what?" He set the box he was carrying on the roof of the car. Maybe he would turn around now. Maybe he would carry it back in the house.

"That you're up to no good." I was ready for him to slap me like Mama slapped him.

But he just said, soft like it was a secret, "You see why

I've to to go, Son. A man can't live in a house of spies."

I wanted to say, I'm *not* a spy! but I *had* watched from the stairs.

"You remember that," Daddy said.

And he walked back to the house for the last load. He had just given me a test. Really I'm supposed to forget what he said. Grown-ups test you sometimes.

You don't know my daddy. He would never call me a spy. He would never go off and leave us. I just have to figure out what to remember, what to forget.

two

So I went in the house to look for Mama and she was in the kitchen peeling peaches. Had the baby on the floor beside her in a wash basket. Mama was wearing her green dress that ties and she had on shoes—I checked that. My mouth was full of questions.

"Don't start," Mama said.

"I'm hungry," I said, which wasn't exactly right. Something was going on in my stomach, though.

"Have a peach," she said.

And I picked one out of the bushel basket. It was warm as the baby's head. I looked around the kitchen: the white cabinets with blue tops Daddy had put in, the yellow curtains Mama had made moving in and out at the window over the sink, breathing like the baby breathes, and just when the peach in my hand started to breathe a little too, Mama reached over, grabbed my shoulder, and shook me. "Don't you have one of your spells this morning! I can't take it!"

"Yes, ma'am," I said, putting the peach on the table and climbing up into a chair. The red-bottomed seat looked like jewels.

"What are you making?" I asked Mama, who had a mountain of peelings and pits on the newspaper in her lap and a roaster full of bald, split peaches on the table.

"Pie," she said.

"How many?"

"Half a bushel of Acuff's finest."

I meant how many *pies,* but I didn't think I should say so. I reached for my peach and bit into it. That peach had so many colors of taste that I forgot what Mama said about not starting and I said, "Sunset."

"What?" Mama asked, without looking up from the newspaper and the knife.

"It tastes like sunset," I said.

Mama looked at me hard. "If you're not careful, Sonny—very, very careful—*you*—" she drew a circle around me in the air with the point of the knife—"are going to be worse than your daddy."

"My daddy's good," I said, putting down the peach, which wasn't good anymore.

"Good for *what* I'd like to know," Mama said.

So I decided to play like I was a statue and see if I was real still if everything else would get real still too. I couldn't stop the fan *click-clacking* overhead, or the curtains whispering at the window, but I could stop the sparks Mama and I were making. They would every one wink out if I turned to stone.

I sat. She peeled. The baby slept. The mountain grew. Then a door opened upstairs and God was sending Loretta to bust up the only good thing I could do.

She did, too, after bounding down the stairs and swinging on the post (it creaked) and hitting the little gong that's on the letter table by the door. She slid into the kitchen in her sock feet, looked at me and Mama at the table, the baby and the bushel of peaches on the floor, and said, "Good Lord! Where's Mamby?"

"Not coming in till this afternoon," Mama told her.

"But I want biscuits," Loretta said.

"You know where the flour is" was all Mama answered.

Loretta got the cornflakes out of the pantry and poured some in a green bowl. She took the lid off the sugar canister and dug out big spoonfuls to sprinkle on the flakes. Then she got the milk bottle out of the Frigidaire.

"See if your brother wants some," Mama said.

"Do you, Sonny?"

I shook my head.

She brought her bowl to the table and started spooning flakes in fast. When there was nothing but a moon of milk left in the bowl, she looked at us again.

"Why are you peeling all those peaches?" she asked.

"For a pie," Mama said. The baby whimpered.

"Who's coming?" Loretta asked.

"Well, I don't know," Mama said, dropping another split peach into the pan. She looked up then, not at us or anything in the room, and said, "I just know who's gone."

three

Loretta made us lunch—Miracle Whip on light bread—and then Mamby showed up. I wanted to stay in the kitchen but Mama sent us straight upstairs.

"She's telling about Daddy," Loretta said, sitting on the clothes hamper in the hall. It's the best place to listen if you're scared to sit on the stairs. We couldn't hear anything, though.

In a little while Mama brought Deaton—the baby's name was Deaton Merrill—up for a nap and said she would lie down too. "Be quiet and don't get in Mamby's way," she said. I followed Loretta downstairs, walking on the carpet next to the wall like Mama told us to make it wear even. Loretta went right down the middle.

Mamby was cleaning up after the peach pie, sweeping flour and peelings into a dustpan.

"Your mama's outdone herself," she said when she saw us standing in the doorway.

"Daddy, too," Loretta said, and I made a yelp like a stepped-on puppy. I didn't mean to.

"Come here to me," Mamby said, putting down broom and dustpan and holding out her arms. I ran over and cried into her apron.

She kept one arm out. "Loretta?"

"No thanks," Loretta said. "I'm busy."

All of Mama's people came over that night: Grandma and Grandpa; Uncle Hickman and Aunt Roo with Jessie and Jocelyn, their girls; Aunt Joy and Uncle Sinclair and Albion, the oldest cousin, and even Great-aunt Toon, who mostly stays in the back room at Grandma's house. She's failing, they say. I asked Loretta how somebody who didn't go to school could be failing and she said, "You are pathetic. It means *dying*." That didn't make sense to me. If she was dying, how could she come to dinner?

Loretta, who is in the fifth grade because she skipped the fourth, is good at school, which she hates. What she loves is Death. So after she studied on my question, she smiled and said, "Actually, Sonny, she's flunking out of the School of Life." Loretta keeps a notebook full of Last Words, which she likes to read from, especially when we have company. And this night, the night of the day Daddy left us, the night of enough peach pie to feed all of Crenshaw County, she brought her book to the table and, right after Grandpa's blessing, read, "Stonewall Jackson was dying of a battle wound when he said, 'Let us cross over the river and rest in the shade of the trees.'"

"Very peaceful," Grandma said.

"Do you suppose he saw Jordan?" Aunt Joy asked.

"More likely a river of blood," Grandpa said. "The man's work was slaughter."

"And his next-to-last words," Loretta went on, "or next to next-to-last, were 'I have always desired to die on Sunday.'"

"*Was* it Sunday?" I asked.

"'Course it was," Loretta said.

Aunt Roo looked at her, then at Mama, who wasn't looking at anything. Her plate was piled with the ham and potato salad and scalloped pineapple and corn muffins everybody had brought, but she wasn't touching it. "Isn't this talk perhaps a bit"—Aunt Roo wrinkled her forehead—"morbid, Loretta? For the table, I mean."

Loretta closed her notebook.

"The child has a sense of history," Grandpa said. "I'm proud of that."

"But perhaps"—Aunt Roo's hair was trembling now—"last words, Papa, tonight—"

Before Grandpa could reply, Mama stood up. Her napkin fell into her plate. "It's BUSINESS," she said. "Leon has gone to Natchez on Delta Paper Mill business and don't any of you forget it!"

"No, Selma, of course—," Grandma started, but Mama walked out into the hall. We heard the front door open.

"You go after her, Joy," Grandma urged, and Aunt Joy scooted her chair back from the table.

"Leave her be," Grandpa ordered, and she scooted back in. Then he turned his eyes on me. "You going to eat, Sonny? Or are you going to dry up and blow away?"

"Eat," I said. I had already tasted the scalloped pineapple, my favorite, and a bit of corn muffin, and now I took a bite of the ham. It tasted sweet and pink. One little strip I couldn't chew, though. My teeth bounced off it. So I took it out of my mouth and put it on my plate.

"Help my time!" Aunt Roo exclaimed. "Sonny, where are your manners?"

"In the grease can," Loretta answered.

"Hush," Aunt Roo told her, then said, "Put that back in your mouth, Sonny. Don't make a face at me!"

I put the lumpy stringy soft something back on my tongue. It hollered down to everything else I had eaten.

"Now here's what you do when, for whatever reason, you have something in your mouth you cannot swallow." She lifted her napkin in front of her mouth, held it a minute, folded it toward her face, and put it back on her lap. "See?" she said.

"What?" I asked.

"Ooooh!" Loretta squealed. "I saw it on his tongue!"

All the girls giggled and Albion laughed out loud.

Aunt Roo ignored them. "I hid it in my napkin," she said. Her cheeks were getting pink as her ruffle-collared dress. "You try, Sonny."

So I did. I put my napkin in front of my face, opened my mouth, and began pushing the ham thing out with my tongue. The trouble was it got stuck where my baby tooth fell out and when I tried to get it loose, I touched my napkin to my tongue and everything in my stomach came loose with it. I tried to turn away real fast, but still some got on the tablecloth.

"Lord have mercy!" Grandma said.

Aunt Joy jumped up and came over to me. "Get a wet washrag, Loretta. You started this." And then, "Roo, you should be ashamed of yourself. This is not the night to teach this boy manners."

The room was taking me for a ride, and it wasn't my fault. Anybody can upchuck.

"It's this heat," Aunt Joy said as she wiped my face with the washrag.

"Added to the upset," Grandma said.

"Upset, my God!" Grandpa roared. "This boy has been deserted by his daddy!"

"Chester," Grandma said. "Don't."

But he grumbled on. "That's what Selma gets for marrying a man with no people."

"He'll be back, Grandpa." I said, but I wasn't sure if my words were where he could hear. "It's just the paper mill."

"Come on, Sonny," Aunt Joy said. "Let's you go lie down on the kitchen couch." With her arm around my shoulder, she guided me out of the dining room through the kitchen and over to the soft old couch, where I lay down. The last thing I heard was Grandma saying, "Let's have our pie in the parlor."

"I don't care for any pie," Grandpa said.

"Well, you've got to eat some," Grandma told him. "Selma's made enough for the whole town."

four

It took a while before Mama acted like Mama again. But Mamby was there part of every day except Sunday, so we got washed and fed. She didn't complain, but I did hear her say to herself one day while she ironed a heap of shirts and shorts and dresses, "Sure does rock the boat when the captain jumps ship."

After a while, Daddy sent money to the bank, and Mama glowed. "See?" she said to us at supper that night. "Your daddy sent his pay home like any man who has to work far off. If he can't come home by next payday, he'll send a letter, too."

He didn't, though. "Maybe we should write to Daddy," I said once when we were having our Saturday morning biscuits and sorghum. The baby was on Mama's lap, mushing crumbs in the sweetness on her plate.

"Oh, yeah," Loretta said. "A friendly letter." With one arm Mama hugged the baby close, and with the other she reached out to smack Loretta on the cheek.

"Don't show yourself, young lady," she said. And that was as far as the letter talk went.

I was sure when a birthday came—or Christmas—that Daddy would come home. But he didn't. Didn't even send a card. Just money. I know now that Mama didn't even know where he was.

Deaton grew anyway. He crawled and wobbled and walked and then talked a blue streak. First it was just "Ma-*ma*-moo-ma-mom-ma!" but soon it was "Bikit" when he was hungry and "Picka up!" when he woke and "Redda bye?" when Loretta was gone to school.

He never said "Daddy," though, and that bothered me. So I tried to teach him. I showed him the picture of Daddy in his Air Force uniform that hung over the piano. "That's our daddy," I said, dragging Deaton about a foot off the ground, which was as high as I could get him. "Look," I said. "Sonny's daddy, Retta's daddy, Deaton's daddy."

"Sonday," he said, smiling.

"He doesn't know what a daddy is," I complained to Mamby.

"That's good," she said. "Long as he don't know, then he don't know what he ain't got."

And we left it at that. Until spring. Until Uncle Marty came.

It was what the One-Way Word of Faith Tabernacle called a Soul-Winning Visitation. Or, as Uncle Marty himself put it, extending the Right Hand of Fellowship to the Lapsed and the Lost. Loretta said, "But what if you're left-handed?" which she is.

Mama said we must be the Lapsed, because our names were still on the roll at the First Methodist. We just hadn't gone back since Daddy had been "transferred."

That's what she was calling it by June, when Uncle Marty showed up.

He didn't come by himself. A big flowered woman was with him. "I'm Mrs. Pastor Biggs," she said, holding out a hot plump hand, "and this is Martin Bonner."

I didn't shake her hand, but she pushed the hair back from my forehead, so I felt it. And Uncle Marty's, too, when he rested it on the top of my head.

"Leon's boy," he said, like this was a surprise. "You're Leon's boy."

I liked that. And I was hugging it to myself, thinking how I was Daddy's boy but Deaton was only his baby, when Loretta said, "You're the Donut Man!"

"Praise God, I am, Little Missy," Uncle Marty said, reaching to pat her head.

"And at your store you make people pray before they can have one bite," she went on.

He snatched his hand back. "That's not true," Mrs. Pastor Biggs said.

"No," said Uncle Marty. "I just print the Word on the menu. 'A lamp unto their feet and a light unto their path.'"

Loretta started to say something back but Mama jerked her hair ribbon. "Won't you all sit awhile?" she said, stretching her arm out toward the chairs. They did, and Mama went to the kitchen and brought back sweet tea.

Then Uncle Marty talked about the fire of God.

And Mrs. Pastor Biggs talked about the light.

And Uncle Marty talked about the need of Saved Souls to gather as a flock.

And Mrs. Pastor Biggs talked about Sunday school.

And this went on long past all the different kinds of donuts I could think of to entertain myself with. Finally Uncle Marty said, "Well, Mrs. Bradshaw, do you think you might bring these fine children and worship with us soon?"

"I just might," Mama said.

"He supports us in our hour of darkness," Mrs. Pastor Biggs said. I looked out the window. The fireflies weren't blinking yet.

It was a while before I found out the One-Way folks

didn't talk about stuff you could see. And by then Uncle Marty had long since become the next best thing to a Bradshaw. Our play-daddy, Deaton called him, after he became part of our lives. But that first time, Deaton just looked at him and grinned his tooth-starter grin. "Sonday!" he called out.

five

I didn't want to go to church, but if we had to, I wanted to go back to the Methodists, where I could lean against Grandma and hear Grandpa snore, and where the people who wanted to love on you after the service sometimes gave you peppermints.

But Mama was determined to try One-Way. "They reached out to us," she said, standing in the living room, squishing the curtains she had made onto the rod.

"Viruses reach out to you too," Loretta said.

Mama looked stony. "What the Lord had in mind when He made your mouth, I do not know."

That would have stung me like a hornet, but Loretta brushed it off. "At least there'll be a show," she said, and walked out the front door. I followed. She went to the driveway, climbed up, and sat on the trunk of the car. We weren't allowed to do that.

"What kind of show do they have?" I asked.

"Who?"

"That church Mama wants to go to."

"Oh, I'm not talking about *them,* though I hope they throw snakes and roll around like tumbleweed. I'm talking about Grandpa."

"Is he going?"

"Sonny, sometimes I think the Rural Electric hasn't got as far as your brain yet. Grandpa wouldn't go to One-Way if Jesus was preaching. But Mama's going to have to tell him *we're* going, and then there'll be fireworks for sure."

"Fire—?" I started, but Loretta put one hand on my head and then hit it with her other fist.

"See if that gets the lights on," she said, then scooted down off the Buick and ran around the garage to the backyard. I followed, but when I saw she was climbing the pine tree, I gave up and went in the back door. Anybody knows better than to get up a tree with Loretta.

It happened to be the week that Grandpa robbed the bees, and Mama and Aunt Roo and Aunt Joy went over to help Grandma get the honey into jars. Mama wanted Loretta there this time so she could learn how it was done ("Useless information," said Loretta), and I wanted to go because jarring the honey is an even bigger, sweeter mess than Christmas baking.

No matter how hard everybody tries to *be careful*—wipe drips, pay attention, look before they pour—there is always a moment when an amber lake of honey flows to the edge of Grandma's white enamel kitchen table and begins to string itself down to the floor. And some years an aunt will be cutting the comb to fit the quart jars—they don't put comb in the little jars— and a chunk will break free and skitter across the table and maybe ricochet off the stove or refrigerator, shooting out honey when it hits and dropping to the blue swirls of Grandma's linoleum. Then Lady, Grandma's Chihuahua, taps in on her toenails to sniff and maybe lick it once before Grandma grabs her up and wipes her feet off with a rag.

All this is plenty of entertainment for me, plus every so often I get spoonfuls of honey. But this year there was more. Grandma had barely got the jars boiled when Mama said quietly, "I've decided to take the children to the One-Way Word of Faith Tabernacle this Sunday."

"Oh Selma, no!" said Aunt Joy like Mama had said she'd come down with some bad sickness.

"Yes," said Mama.

"It's a free country," Loretta said.

"Not in this house," Aunt Roo put in. "I'm afraid you have to pay."

"Why?" I asked.

"Is that wise?" Aunt Joy asked, her face in a worry frown, honey running from her wrists to her elbows.

"I worry about your daddy's heart," Grandma said.

Mama got red in the face. "He's not going to have a heart attack just because I try out a new church!"

"You don't know that," Aunt Joy said.

"The doctor told him anything could do it, any shock."

"And Selma, you don't want to—," Aunt Roo started.

"LIFE is shocking," Mama cut in. "He's just got to take his chances."

"Selma Estelle, I'm ashamed of you!" Grandma declared, her blue eyes looking fierce at Mama. Mama gave her the same look back. "You tell him yourself then. I won't bear the responsibility."

"All right," Mama said. "Where is he?"

"He's resting after his constitutional."

Loretta, holding a block of comb above the glass mouth of a jar, looked at me. "She means his walk."

I nodded. Mama grabbed a dish towel and headed for the bedroom, just the other side of the dining room.

"Come back and wash!" Grandma demanded. "You'll leave a trail of honey."

But Mama kept going.

"She's going to sweeten him up," Loretta said.

Then the kitchen was like the castle after Sleeping

Beauty fell under the spell. Nobody moved. Nobody spoke. Honey made its slow golden way down fingers into jars, onto aprons.

Till Grandpa roared, "Good God Almighty!" and I breathed again. Bedsprings screaked and the floor creaked under his weight as he stood. "Haven't you put this family through enough? You couldn't keep your husband and now—"

"Daddy—" Mama's voice sounded thick.

"Now you want to go humiliate us at some Holy Roller church. Next thing we know you'll be foaming at the mouth. What kind of fool are you?"

Mama stormed back into the kitchen, grabbed the baby out of the high chair, and made us leave without even washing our hands. She kept flexing hers as she drove. I could feel them stick to the steering wheel.

Loretta, in the front seat, was wordless for once. I sat in the back with Deaton. We were almost home before Mama spoke. "I should have said 'My own!'" she told the windshield. "'My own kind of fool!'"

When we got in the house, Mama said, "I've got to go lie down. Loretta, you give Deaton a sponge bath." I was hoping to slip into my room when she added, "And Sonny, you take a damp rag and get that honey out of the car."

Part Two

1954

six

That honey Sunday was the beginning of our new life.
Everything had sort of stopped when Daddy left, or moved
real slow around the empty places in our house, but once
Mama took up at One-Way, things started moving again—
and in a different direction. The biggest change was having Uncle Marty around so much. He and Mama got to be
real good friends and, since he was a bachelor with no
family in Mozier, he ate with us several nights a week. He
never stayed late, but while Loretta was doing the dishes
he and Mama would sit out on the porch "where if it was
ever going to get cool it would be cool" and talk.

I never asked Mama what they talked about, but she
was always saying "I'll ask Marty about that" when she was
worried about money or had a problem with the water heater

or the Buick's trunk wouldn't close. I don't know if Uncle Marty really helped her with this stuff or she just needed somebody to talk to. She had those brothers, of course, but they were bossy, like Grandpa, and anyway, once she struck out on her own to go to One-Way, she didn't depend on them so much.

Time went along. We all got bigger and more like ourselves. I got obsessed with airplanes. The summer I was thirteen I wanted money bad. All I could think about was building models—some ships and cars, but mostly airplanes. Mostly warplanes, like Daddy flew in over Europe. I loved everything about building models: the cellophane coming off the box like a shirtsleeve, the wings and tail and fuselage pieces all nested inside. I loved the slow process, fitting and gluing and waiting, knowing I had everything I needed. Then dipping the brush in a pool of silver, laying on the decals, and finally setting the finished plane on the shelf Mama let me build in the room I shared with Deaton and his new kitten, Cantaloupe. The shelf was high as my shoulder and went around three walls.

There were only two problems with the models: money and Deaton. Too much Deaton, who wanted "just to hold" the models, and not enough of what it took to buy the kits. Money stayed scarce, though Mama had a job by then at Boykin's Jewelry and Hardware, and we had sold the big house on Magnolia and moved to a little one on Rhubarb.

"Imagine ending up in a starter home!" Aunt Roo had said when we moved, but I liked it. White Pine Creek ran right behind our house on its way to the Conecuh River, and I could wade and wander by myself or slap together mud dams and catch crawdads with Deaton.

Mama said Daddy still sent the same sum of money even though we were older and needed a lot more things. Loretta had a job three days a week at the Chat 'n' Chew Cafe, and I wanted a job too. I told Mama I'd give her half my pay, just like Retta did.

I started out mowing lawns. I had ten customers, so I would do five a week. This was working well until one Wednesday in late June that was so hot and humid it felt like I was pushing the mower across the bottom of a drained aquarium. I was over at the Rileys'—they have a big corner lot with a little slope to it. About halfway through, I felt a little jerk inside and all the color bleached out of the grass and the mock orange bush I was following the edge of. The next thing I knew the fence was sticking sideways into the clouds.

That settled it for Mama. "No more mowing," she said. "You start those spells again and you could cost us way more than you'll make."

"Yes, ma'am," I said. I hadn't had a spell for two years and was hoping I'd grown out of them. "But what can I do for work?" I asked.

"I'll ask Uncle Marty," she said.

That night at dinner Mama explained what had happened and, between bites of fried corn and stewed tomatoes and piccalilli, Uncle Marty said, "Tell you what, Selma. Why don't you send Sonny to me? I could use some help in the afternoons, cleaning up from the morning and preparing for the morrow. What do you say, Sonny?"

"Thanks, sir," I said, though I figured it would be way hotter than the Rileys' yard in that little dairy stand restaurant where all those donuts were fried and Uncle Marty was puffed up with the Holy Spirit.

Mama looked at me. "That's hot work too," she said.

"But not much exertion," Uncle Marty said. "And there's work he could do in the evening, too."

"What?" we both said at once.

"Well, I've been wanting to make a clean menu board for the front. What I've got now's been scratched out and written over and some of the Scripture's peeled off."

"Sonny's got a steady hand to paint," Mama said.

"If you want warplanes," Loretta put in.

Uncle Marty ignored her. "That's what I know," he said.

But Retta wouldn't be ignored. "He's got a quick hand for grabbing donuts, too," she said. She meant from the pile of leftovers Uncle Marty always brought us on

Saturday nights. The Circle of Life was closed on Sunday.

"I'll deduct them from his pay," Uncle Marty said.

So the very next day I got started working for Uncle Marty. I wasn't allowed to wait on people, either at the walk-up or at the six little tables inside. "It's not that you wouldn't do a good job of it, Sonny," Uncle Marty explained, resting his hand on my shoulder blade. "*You* do a good job of everything. It's just that waiting on folks is part of my ministry."

What he meant was he sized up the customers and then greeted them with whatever Bible verse seemed appropriate. Local folks were used to it. They could take "Whither can I flee from Thy spirit?" with a half-dozen plain glazed or "Thou knowest not the day nor the hour" with four éclairs and two fritters. Only strangers were likely to take offense, and Mozier didn't get many of those. But I do remember a woman the first week shoving her hamburger and fries back through the window before Uncle Marty could finish intoning, "Yea, though I walk through the valley of the shadow of death . . ." She fled, and he ate the burger in two bites.

Never skinny, Uncle Marty had blimped up in the years we'd known him. Now that I worked for him—scrubbing the donut trays and icing tubs, the dough hooks and the grill—I could see why. Not only did he eat food the heathen refused, he ate all the sweet kitchen failures: broken donuts, cream puffs that didn't seal. He forgave himself all his shortcomings as a cook, or at least he hid the evidence. It made me gag, but when I told Mama, she just said, "I guess that's why he's so sweet."

seven

By the time I arrived around ten each morning—it turned out that I worked morning *and* afternoon—the major frying and glazing and sugaring were done and Uncle Marty glistened. Oily, sticky, crystallized he was, and all he washed were his hands before he commenced to mixing the two doughs that would go in the cooler till 4 A.M., when it was time to make out the donuts for the next day's frying.

After a week of letting me do nothing but dishwashing and floor sweeping, he finally remembered the menu board.

"Make a sketch first," he cautioned, "so you can get the spacing right. Even if you don't have room for the whole verse on there, you need to get enough to catch the interest of the heathen and trigger the faithful's memory.

Those who need to can look it up when they get home."

He was dead serious and covered with flour when he said this, since his apron only protected a small portion of his big front and he never could keep all the flour in the bowl.

The old menu board had loaves and fishes painted everywhere and every which way on it. I told Uncle Marty I thought this was confusing. "You don't sell bread and fish," I reminded him.

His floury eyebrows came together in a scowl. "Everybody knows about the feeding of the five thousand, Sonny."

"Sure," I said. "But they're coming here for *food,* not preaching, so when they see bread and fish, they think that's what you sell."

"Oh," said Uncle Marty. "Ummmm." He looked at the board, which I had propped up on a worktable. "I can't think what else to use," he admitted.

"What about the vine and branches?" I asked, amazed that I remembered Pastor Biggs's Sunday text.

"Praise the Lord, yes," Uncle Marty said, reaching out to pat my shoulder, then taking back his floury paw. "'I am the vine and ye are the branches.' Sonny, you are a genius! I do declare this is the work you were born for."

I hope not, I thought, but what I said was "Thanks. I'll get to work."

I sketched the vine to grow up from the bottom edge and branch out to either side, making a big U. It looked like the glockenspiel Brenda Lewis played in the school band, only green. And I drew the words coming down the outside of one branch—*I am the vine*—and climbing up the other—*and ye are the branches.*

The old menu board had been added onto wherever a new item would fit, so Onion Rings was right next to Banana Split, and Chili Cheese Fries was up by Vanilla Coke. I thought Chili Cheese Fries should be taken off completely in consideration for those who might have to watch somebody eat them, but Uncle Marty said, "This isn't your grandmother's table, Sonny. We're not selling manners."

That was for sure. The day before I started on the menu board I had watched a man—Granville Sims, in fact—flick a kidney bean from his sleeve into his mouth.

Anyway, I asked Uncle Marty if it was okay for me to rearrange and sort out the menu items and he said, "Sure. Just don't mix up the Scripture."

"Okay," I said, though I couldn't see why it mattered. Why is "O set me upon the rock that is higher than I" more suitable for a hot dog than a hamburger? Why does chocolate chip ice cream rate "I know that my redeemer liveth"?

Halfway through the sketch, a thought hit me. Why not

put "Ask and it shall be given" at the top of the board? That would tie the menu notion and the Scripture notion together. So I suggested this to Uncle Marty, who had left the realm of flour and begun chopping onions.

His face went blank for a second and then, for the first time I ever saw, his face got red and he was furious. "It's one thing to mock *me,* Sonny Bradshaw," he said, wiping an onion tear from his cheek with the back of his chopping hand so that only his glasses kept the knife blade out of his eye. "I'm a man, fat and fallen, and that does not matter. But to mock the open arms of the Lord, to equate His grace with donuts and fries is more than I will abide."

"But Uncle Marty, that's not what I—"

"Hush! I don't want to hear any more out of you!"

Where did *that* come from? I wondered, stung. At the same time I thought, while lettering in burgers and Bible verses, "To equate His grace with *grease*" would have been a better line.

eight

When Uncle Marty paid me for my first two weeks' work, I put
that together with my mowing money and bought a B-17
bomber model at the dime store. This was the plane
Daddy had flown in over France. He was the navigator. I
was going to build it just perfect to show him. In case he
ever came back.

The B-17 was the most expensive and complicated
model I'd tried, so Mama got the idea that I needed Uncle
Sinclair to help me build it. I didn't want help, especially
not from him. He's a plumber and he may be good at
pipes, but he's not a careful person. The parts of a model
are thin and delicate. You can't go at them with a wrench.

"Honest, Mama, I can do it on my own," I said, but it
was no use. Mama wants me to be close to Uncle Sink.

(Folks call him Sink, on account of his job, but she says it's not respectful, so we can't say it out loud.)

"I like to see my boy learning from my big brother," Mama said. What she means is, she thinks I need a fake daddy. "A man's guiding hand," I heard her tell Aunt Joy, which is probably why she has Uncle Marty over to dinner too, but it's stupid, if you ask me. I don't want to be guided by either one of them.

Still, Uncle Sink arrived Saturday afternoon to help. Mama had put newspaper on the table in the kitchen and set out a bowl with a wet rag in it. I had separated the parts and laid them out by size, not wanting Uncle Sink to break any. I had the glue tube out too, but not the paint and decals. We wouldn't need them till the next day.

"Hey, Sonny!" Uncle Sink exclaimed as he came into the kitchen. "What have we here?" He stood by the table, hands on his hips, dressed in one of the gray jumpsuits he wears to work. His hair, once reddish gold, is going pale, but his mustache and eyebrows are still so bright they look stuck on.

"It's a B-17," I said. "Like Daddy—"

"Yep, that's what he flew, all right," Uncle Sink said, rushing past any chance to talk about Daddy. "Let's see. . . ." He picked up pieces of the fuselage and tried to fit them together.

"Here are the directions," I said, handing him the folded white paper.

"Oh, I know how to do this," he said, putting the paper down. "Don't worry."

And without a minute's consideration, he twisted the top off the glue and got to work.

"It goes step by step," I said.

"That's for if you don't know how to do it," he insisted.

I stood disbelieving as he slathered on the glue and pressed the two biggest pieces together. I'd never get the seats and the people in the cockpit now.

"Better let that dry," he said when he finished the fuselage. "That's the hard part. When that's done, we'll come back and do the wings."

I watched the glue ooze out between the joints and despaired. Maybe you can do pipes like that and it doesn't matter. Who looks at pipes?

I reached over with my rag to wipe it off.

"Don't touch it till it sets!" Uncle Sink warned. "You'll ruin the alignment."

"I just want to wipe off the glue," I explained.

"Too late," he said.

I turned my head away.

"It's okay, Son. You can paint over it."

Yeah, I thought, and I know how that will look. But I didn't say anything.

"Sinclair," Mama said, coming in the back door from taking down the wash. "Would you like a piece of buttermilk pie? I made it yesterday."

He smiled and patted his belly, which was just the least bit round. "You don't have to ask twice," he said.

Mama set the clothes basket down and opened the Frigidaire. She took out the pie and put it on the counter. "You want some too, Sonny?" she asked.

"No," I said. I felt all glued shut.

"No, what?" Mama asked.

"No, thank you."

"That's better. Sinclair, why don't we go sit on the porch? It's got to be cooler than this."

So we did. Loretta was already out there with one foot propped against the banister, painting her toenails fire-engine red.

"My stars, Loretta. Why do you want to go painting yourself up?" Mama asked.

"Like some war-whoop Indian," Uncle Sink added.

"'I dwell in possibility,'" Loretta said.

"What does that mean?" Uncle Sink asked, balancing his pie plate while lowering himself to the glider.

"She dwells in a pigsty," Mama said. "You should see her room."

"It's a quotation," Loretta put in. "From a *poem*."

"When I was your age," Mama said, "they taught us, 'Build thee more stately mansions, O my soul.'"

Loretta was twisting around to reach her little toe, so I couldn't see her face when she said, "My stately mansion includes red toenails."

"Does she remind you of anybody?" Uncle Sink asked Mama.

"Every day of this world," Mama said. I knew they meant Daddy. Anything they didn't like about any of us kids got dealt to him. Which was the same as the discard pile.

Mama wasn't having pie or sitting on the glider with me and her big brother. She was perched on the watermelon-colored metal chair she called the Tulip Chair and fanning herself with a cardboard-on-a-stick from the One-Way Word of Faith Tabernacle. On it was a picture of Jesus knocking at the door.

"I don't see how you can do that, Sis," Uncle Sink said. He calls her Sis when he's teasing.

"And why not?" she asked.

"It says 'One-Way,' and you're going back and forth to beat the band."

Uncle Sink and his family—in fact, all of Mama's people—still went to the First Methodist, and they were suspicious of Uncle Marty's church. I didn't call it *our* church, though Pastor Biggs had dunked Deaton in the river three times so he'd have a ticket to Heaven. As a baby I'd been sprinkled by the Methodists, and that was as wet as I intended to get.

"Where's Deaton?" I asked.

"Albion's pitching to him down at the park," Mama said.

Albion? All Albion ever did was press down the keys on his saxophone and take Lena McWhorter on dates in his daddy's car. He couldn't throw a ball straight to save him.

"Deaton will be slugging a lot of air," Loretta said.

Uncle Sink laughed. And Mama said nothing. She'd have fumed if I'd said that. It beats me how Loretta got a license for her tongue.

"Let's go, Son," Uncle Sink said. "Pie's all gone and the glue's bound to be dry now."

"I'll take that," Mama said, reaching for the pastry-flaked plate.

"You outdid yourself, Selma," he said, and Mama beamed.

Back in the hot little kitchen, Uncle Sink told me, "You do it this time, Sonny. You assemble the wings."

"But you left out—," I started, wanting to say I knew it wouldn't work.

But he cut in. "I know you can do it. You've done all those others. And your hand would be steadier than mine."

Not just my hand, I thought. My mind is steadier. Would you take apart a pipe without knowing what it's hooked up to? Without cutting off the water? I wanted to ask. But I didn't. I gritted my teeth and glued the wing halves together. Maybe I was wrong. Maybe Uncle Sink knew something.

nine

The One-Way Word of Faith Tabernacle is a cinder block building about a mile out the Andalusia Road. They built it there because Sister Sarvis, who never married and is as old as dirt, gave the church part of her farm in exchange for looking after her till the angels take her home. That was ten years ago, so she got a good deal.

Until then, the One-Way met at the American Legion Hall in Andalusia. But Uncle Marty said that after Saturday night parties, that space was "far from sanctified." It was far from most people's houses, too, so they jumped at the chance to build close.

The first Sunday we went there, that summer after Leon left, I thought the folding chairs and general bareness were because One-Way was new and poor. I thought as soon as they could afford it, they'd do better—put in pews and carpet and a carved Lord's Supper table like the Methodists. But no, they *believe* in linoleum and metal chairs and a beat-up podium that could have come out of some closed-down high school. For communion, they have squished pellets of white bread and grape drink in paper cups, and for baptizing they walk to the back of their land and wade right out into the Conecuh River. Or, if they're feeble, someone drives them down the rutted road.

Anyway, I have got used to how the church looks and how people sometimes shout and fall down during the service. At first that made me feel like I had a floor burn all over, but now it's like flies buzzing. And I have got used to Mama singing LOUD and even holding her arms up sometimes, which she never would do if any of her kin were around. When Deaton was a baby and Sister Clemons started playing "Jesus Paid It All," or "Love Lifted Me," Mama would hand him, squirming or sleep-heavy, to me and say, "You take the baby, Sonny. I've got to praise."

What I haven't got used to is what happens to Uncle Marty at One-Way. He's an Elder, so he gets to read the Word and pray and help dunk the Saved in the river. But unlike Pastor Biggs, who is his same fake self all the time, who talks in this slippery way like he's been drinking bubble bath, and who mostly preaches "Get baptized or get burned," Uncle Marty gets transformed. I don't know what else to call it. Watching him at our house during the week or at the Circle of Life once I started working for him, I would think I must have imagined how he is on Sunday, but then the Lord's Day would roll around and it would happen again.

The Sunday of the airplane building, stuck between Mama and Loretta, I tried to think past the fight they had before we left—Mama wanted Retta to wear a sweater to protect the faithful from her bony shoulders in a sundress—so I could picture each piece of my B-17 and figure out how to save it from Uncle Sink. I had no intention of listening to Uncle Marty. But while I can stare straight ahead during Pastor Biggs's sermons, or Elder Jamison's prayers, Uncle Marty's prayer voice puts a hand at the back of my neck so my eyes close, my head bows, and like it or not, I hear every word.

"Jesus," he started off, "Jesus, Jesus," like he was testing, tasting the name:

> son of David, Mary's boy, we know You're
> our brother. We know You walked roads just
> as crooked and dusty as ours. Alabama!
> Yes, Lord, and Galilee! And we know You're
> here among us, eating at our table, sweating
> in cotton fields and paper mills, feeding

babies and hanging the wash on the line.
You walk with us, Jesus, and we praise
You—

"Yes, Lord!" someone called out.

We thank You for every fish we catch and
every tomato we break off the vine.
And Jesus

"Tell Him, Brother!"

Jesus, Jesus, we ask You to put Your hands
in our hands. Reach out, Lord, through us
right here in Mozier.

"Here, Lord!"

Let the fire of Your Gospel shine in us.

"Shine!"

Let it burn in us till the path before us
is so clear we could no more stray from
it than we could grow scales and fins and
gills and live in the deep.

Yet if we did, even if we *did*, Lord,

"Even so!"

                            "Even then!"

      we know You would find us. You went
      to Hell to get us, Lord, went to the Cross,
      and we know there is no place we can
      get into, however deep, however dark,
      that Your love won't find us, won't
      bring us out.
        Blessed Savior, above the dust
      of Mozier, we hear redemption's wings!
                 Amen

"Amen!" The cry went up and bounced all around the room. "Amen! Amen!"

I opened my eyes and saw Mama dabbing at hers with a handkerchief. I didn't cry, but I always felt unsettled after Uncle Marty's prayers—like I'd been somewhere and didn't know how to get back. Other people besides Mama felt something like that too, I could tell; not Loretta—she's too knotty—and not Deaton—he's too young—but Brother and Sister Dillard in front of us, and the Slushers just down the row. They were the only folks I could really look at without being rude, and their mouths were wobbly, their eyes blinking fast. They must *like* this scooted-over feeling, I thought, or they wouldn't come back.

Well, that's because they don't have spells. Let this kind of thing happen to them when they didn't dress up and go looking for it, and they'd be singing a different tune. As it was, the piano notes started rolling, and they opened their grateful mouths and sang:

> I love to tell the Story
> Of unseen things above,
> Of Jesus and His glory,
> Of Jesus and His love.
> I love to tell the Story
> Because I know 'tis true.
> It satisfies my longing
> As nothing else can do.

ten

After church, the whole family had a pot roast dinner at Aunt Roo's. Her rose garden is right outside the dining room window, so for noses at that table there was a battle between roses and roast. Even with the big electric fan over the table, sweat beaded up on us like it did on the iced tea glasses, but still we shoveled in the fuel. I was relieved when Uncle Sink swallowed his last bite of rhubarb pie and said, "Sonny, what do you say we go finish that B-17?" At least it would be cooler at our house, since nobody had been there cooking.

Uncle Sink didn't cool off, though. He didn't slow down, either. Marched right into Mama's kitchen, where I had laid out the parts before church, and started squeezing on glue without even testing the fit of the wings. When he finally realized there was too much glue in the slot where the wing should go, he had a mess on his hands. "Damn thing won't go in," he said, pressing the fragile parts together as if they could be forced.

"I know. But I can get a knife and trim off the glue," I said.

"You do that," Uncle Sink said. I could tell he was peeved. While I was hunting for the right size blade, he pawed through the remaining parts on the table. "What's this?" he asked.

I turned around to see him holding the one-piece cockpit interior.

"It goes in the cockpit," I told him.

"Well, it's a fine time to be telling me," Uncle Sink said, color rising in his face.

"I tried to—," I started.

"You *what*?" he said, looking up at me with sparks in his blue eyes.

"I tried to tell you."

"Like hell you did," he said. "You sat right there and watched me labor over this and never said a word."

"But I did—"

"So don't try to make up some story now after you've wasted my weekend and your fool money!" He stood up and threw the model pieces on the table. "You're just like Albion," he said. "Think you know everything. He wants to play a saxophone the rest of his life. You want to build war toys. Why, I wasn't much older than you two when I was IN the war. Not playing. I jumped *out* of planes like this, Sonny, so don't tell me how they go together. You don't know a thing. Not a thing." He turned and walked out the back door.

Deaton followed him. "You mean you had a parachute?" he asked.

Mama was washing dishes at Aunt Roo's and Loretta was out with her friend Mazelyn, so I had the silence to myself. I took a wing in each hand and squeezed hard, thinking I'd crush them, but they were sturdier than that. Then I went outside and put them on the second of the three concrete steps. Came back in and got the fuselage, too. I was fixing to stomp on them when Deaton came around the driveway side of the house. A red handprint blazed on the side of his face.

"Did he hit you?" I asked.

He nodded. And before I could offer comfort or curse Uncle Sink, Deaton ran up, grabbed one wing, and shielded the other pieces with his arm. "Don't bust it, Sonny!" he said, tears in his voice. "We'll get some *un*glue and start over."

eleven

On Friday afternoon at the end of my fourth week working for him, Uncle Marty was counting money from the register to put in the zippered leather First National pouch when he said, "Sonny, you man the fort while I go put this in the bank."

"Yes, sir," I said, and he paid me what I'd earned and walked, pouch in hand, out the back door to head up Stapleton Street.

There were no customers in sight, I'd done all the scrubbing, and it was so hot I was about to fall asleep.

Not wanting to do that, I looked in the drawer for some paper and something to draw airplanes with. I thought I'd seen a sheet or two when Uncle Marty took out the pouch.

At first all I found were supply order sheets. I couldn't

draw on those, so I kept digging. There was an appointment calendar from the Holtzclaw Insurance Agency. Sometimes they had blank pages at the back, so I opened it up to see, and a letter fell out.

Ordinarily I would have put it back in the drawer without even looking at it—I am not a snoop. But the way the *B* in *Martin Bonner* was drawn looked so familiar that I turned the envelope over just to see who the letter was from, and when it didn't say, I took the single sheet out to check the signature. Before my eyes got to that, though, a sentence jumped out at me: *Tell me what kind of worker Sonny is. . . .* And then I had that feeling you get after you trip but before you fall. I knew I'd find at the bottom of the page the word that was missing from our life: *Leon.*

I shook my head hard. I pulled my hair and bit my tongue and ran water on my left hand.

When things were steady again I looked at the top of the letter for a return address. *1621 Orbison Street, Mobile, Alabama,* it said. Simple as that. Mobile, just down the road. I'd never been there, but it wasn't too far. People went there on the bus. Some even went and came back in the same day. I could do it. I had money. Marty had just given it to me. And I had an address. There was nothing to keep me from finding Daddy now.

I tore a long piece off the cash register tape and copied his address onto it. Then I put the letter back in the calendar, the calendar back in the drawer, and took off running out the back door.

twelve

I knew there was a bus to Mobile but I couldn't catch it in Mozier, where you bought a ticket at the drugstore and waited at the stop on Main Street. Everybody would know who I was and want to know where I was going.

So I ran home, slipped my bike out of the garage, started down the driveway, and realized I had better leave a note. I tore off a piece of the register tape and wrote, bearing on the house:

> Dear All,
> Gone for a couple of days. Do not worry.
> Love,
> Sonny

I stuck this between the back screen and the doorframe. Then I rode over to the drugstore where the schedule was posted, and pedaled as fast as I could for Andalusia. It was so hot that the air coming off the pavement was like dragon breath. Never mind, never mind, I told myself with each turn of the wheel. It doesn't matter.

What mattered was getting to Andalusia and finding a bus station. What mattered was making the 6:55 bus. Which I did, after hiding my bike in some brush grown up around an abandoned house.

The trip to Mobile took two hours, which meant that even in high summer it would be about dark when I got there. And I'd never been to Mobile. I'd never been anywhere. I didn't have a clue where to go. I didn't want to look for Daddy in the dark—I'd never find him, just lose myself.

Well, where do people stay away from home? I asked myself.

Relatives? That was out.

Hotels? Not on donut money.

Churches? Maybe. But what if somebody there wanted to know my name and where I came from? They'd be sure to get in touch with Mama.

Stewing over this whole thing on the swaying bus put me to sleep, and it was only when the bus driver slowed suddenly as we came into town that I woke up. And it *wasn't* a town, it was a CITY, with wide streets and big buildings, and a bay full of ships. I hadn't come to *see* anything. I was looking for Daddy. But still I felt filled up by how beautiful it was, how different it felt from home. No wonder Daddy wanted to live here, I thought—but if he loved the city, why didn't he bring us with him?

By the time I'd walked into the bus station, an ache had got hold of my chest, and I wasn't sure what to do next. I went to the bathroom, then walked over to the bulletin board by the ticket office. It was filled with ads and church times and notices about lost stuff. I couldn't help but read them. In Mozier, I'd know who these people were, but here I didn't, so it was sort of like reading a story. There were lost-and-founds ("One rug, body size, bright stripes, lost here"); rooming house ads and hotel ads; personal notes ("J. V., if you see this, I might be at Starla's. Marybelle"); and then, down in the right-hand corner, the thing I needed to see: "Rooms—cheap. By day or week. Safe and clean. No trouble. YMCA." There was even a map. I copied the directions down on the register receipt that had Daddy's address on it and set off.

It was three blocks on the map, but not small-town blocks, city blocks. The farther I walked, the more my Mobile excitement leaked out of my feet. But my belief that I had to find Daddy and make him face me stayed strong. I needed that to keep out the voices of home. I knew Mama would have gone from frantic to hysterical about me being gone by now. Deaton would probably cry and Loretta would be spitting red-hot curses for having to miss a Friday night date on my account. And Uncle Marty would have activated the One-Way prayer chain before setting out in his DeSoto to hunt for me.

Would he figure it out? Would he wonder about what could have made me run away and then remember the letter in the drawer? I didn't think so. If he could think like that, he wouldn't have put the letter there in the first place.

I was walking past a bank and an antique store and a Woolworth's, looking for Thibideaux Street. No, that was St. Ignatius. Did all cities have streets named like that—all fancy, no Maple or Hawthorne or Rhubarb? I passed a hat shop, a jeweler's, a bookstore. It was deep dark now and the wind off the water seemed to fold the dark up and make it deeper between the streetlights. The wind smelled fishy, too. What if I'd copied the map wrong? But no, there it was, Thibideaux St. I turned left by a little restaurant. Just one block straight ahead and I should be there.

It was after hours so I had to press a buzzer, but a man let me in right away. As I followed him up the few steps to the lobby, I realized he was going to ask my name and decided I had better not give it. I had to figure out someone else to be real fast. I didn't have to work at it. I just opened my mind and a whole new name walked in. Brad,

I thought. Brad Fisher. "Brad" was from Bradshaw, I guess, and "Fisher" came from the smell of the air. I signed the register, pressing hard on the pen as if to make what I wrote true. Then I saw I had to put an address down. Decatur, I wrote, just like I really lived there. This was too easy. It made me feel weird, like any minute I'd have a twin brother and a dog.

"Brad?" The man's voice sounded concerned.

"Yes, sir?"

"I asked how long you'll be staying."

"Oh," I said. "Sorry. Two nights, maybe three. How much does it cost?"

"Ten dollars," he said.

"Okay. Can I just pay for one night right now?"

"All right," the man said. "You can have room 25." He gave me the key, which had a chain with a dimpled ball attached to it, and sent me through a door and down a pale blue hallway. My room was on the right. It was blue too, and had a speckled floor, a folding chair, a beat-up desk, and a naked bed with sheets and a blanket at one end, waiting to be put on. Not this night, I thought.

And so, too tired to worry about tomorrow, I closed the door, turned out the light, and slept.

thirteen

I didn't wake up till ten o'clock, and what woke me then was my empty belly. It felt like somebody had laid an icy football on it. For a minute, before I remembered where I was, I expected to walk downstairs and have Mama say, "*You* slept the sleep of the dead!" And if Loretta was around, she'd add, "I'd save it for eternity myself." But there was no Mama, no Loretta, no Deaton wanting me to go outside and pitch. More important at the moment, there was no sorghum and biscuits. I was starving.

I cleaned up as best I could without a shower or fresh clothes and headed out. The same man who'd let me in was at the desk.

"Hope you can find what you're looking for, Brad."

"Thanks," I said a little too late. "You too." Well, that

didn't make any sense, I thought, but it got me out the door.

I needed food and a map. The Y probably had a map, but I was too hungry to go back. If I could just find the restaurant I'd walked by the night before . . . I retraced my steps.

The morning air was thick and sweet—Alabama summer with the bay and the paper mills thrown in. If I could just add the smell of something good I was about to eat, it would be perfect. Then I came around the corner and there it was. Not the restaurant I was looking for, but a little cart run by an old man selling rolls and coffee and some kind of pancake things. Bubbles of butter, cinnamon dust, and coffee steam all grabbed my rib cage and hauled me over.

"What's for you?" the old man asked, his words kind of funny.

"A big roll," I told him, pointing. "One of those with the sugar, and coffee."

"Beignet et cafe!" he said, handing me the roll on a little paper plate. I took a bite while he was pouring the coffee.

"You grand guy," he said. "Very hungry."

I nodded.

"Let's give you this also," he said, rolling up one of the buttery pancakes and sliding it into waxed paper. "This is a crêpe," he explained, handing it to me along with the coffee.

"Thank you," I said. "How much?"

"One dollar," he said. Now that I had a few bites in my stomach, I slowed down and looked at him. His white hair was so short and wavy it looked like it was painted on, and his eyes were as blue as the ocean on the map at school.

I gave him the money, knowing he wasn't charging me enough. "Thanks a lot," I said, and started to walk away. But his eyes and the map pulled me back. "Do you know how to get to Orbison Street?" I asked him.

He laughed. *"Orbison,"* he said, like it was in another language. "You take the streetcar?"

"No," I said.

"A long walk then," he said.

"That's okay," I told him.

"Very good," he said. "This is how you go." He took a napkin from his stack and began drawing the route for me. Every time there was a turn, he stopped, squinted into the distance, and then gestured with his arms as though I could see what he was seeing and remember. But I couldn't. I just hoped I could read the napkin.

"Thanks again," I said when he handed me his drawing. "For the food, too."

He smiled. "Go well," he said, and waved.

I had a weird feeling walking away from him, eating

my pillowy roll and drinking bitter coffee. It didn't seem real, him being there and being so friendly, and giving me stuff. And his eyes. . . . I made myself focus on the map and not the strangeness, pulled myself back to my purpose.

Even outlined on a small napkin, the way to Orbison Street looked like a long haul. "Time to lay shoe leather in a line," as Mamby would say. It was a sleepy kind of morning, the air like bathwater. I checked off the streets close to his address: Yazoo, Gibbon, Feltner, Orbison. I walked four or five blocks down Orbison, watching it change from just-painted jewelry and clothing stores to slightly rundown newsstands and bars with doors leading to stairways wedged in between. 1612 . . . 1618 . . . 1621—that was it. Then it was one step up to a door the color of chocolate when it starts to whiten.

Looking through its window, I saw mailboxes inside a little hall that led to the stairs. I didn't think about it being locked, and when I turned the knob, which had a design carved in it and was loose, it swung in with a creak. Stepping inside, I smelled old stuff—cooking, garbage, sweat. I scanned the mailboxes for BRADSHAW but didn't find it. "Number 9," it said on the address, but mailbox 9 said CLAXON. Never mind. It was all I had, so up I climbed. The stairs were painted that chocolate color too, and they had worn-out rubber treads nailed to them. His feet go here, I thought as I went up the two long flights. The first hall was dark, but the second floor had a dirty skylight. Oh well, gritty light was better than none. I found number 9 and knocked.

I waited.

I knocked again.

It was Saturday morning, I suddenly remembered, and people who had worked all week could be sleeping. Who was I to disturb their peace? But then who was Daddy to walk out on us?

I knocked harder.

A man opened the door. Standing there in gray pants and a sleeveless undershirt, he wasn't much taller than me. His hair, including that on his chest, was brown—thick and curly—and his skin was tan, like he worked outside. He had a lot of muscles, too. . . .

"It's early, for God's sake," he said. "What do you want?"

"I want Leon Bradshaw."

"Hoooo!" he said, then called over his shoulder. "Raymond, get in here! Some kid wants"—he sang the word—"Leon."

"Doesn't he live here?" I asked, looking over and around the man, trying to see something familiar in the apartment. But the shades were closed and I could only see dark shapes of furniture.

A thin blond man came up behind the strong one. He had on a robe, pale green, shiny. His mustache parted in the middle like Cantaloupe's whiskers.

"Lord, Lord," the blond man said. "What does he want with Leon?"

To my surprise, I said, "He's my daddy."

The swarthy guy gave a snort. "Been holding out on us!" he said, not to me but to the other man.

"Well, he's not here," the blond one said. "He doesn't live here. He just uses—"

"Watch it," the swarthy guy warned. "What makes you think he lives here?"

"This address," I said, "on a letter."

"To you?" There was a shove in his voice.

"No."

"You been snooping," he said. It wasn't a question.

"We could ask him in," Raymond suggested.

"We could go to jail, too." The doorkeeper stood his ground.

"Jail?"

"Look," he said, holding his left hand out in front of my face and ticking off points finger by finger as he talked. "Leon don't live here"—little finger; "You may or may not be his kid"—ring finger . . .

"He is, though, Eddie. Look at him," Raymond said. His voice was breathy, as if *he* was scared too.

"You've already shown you're a sneak, so we can't trust you"—middle finger; "You ain't where you belong"—skipping to the thumb; "And anyway, we just mail things for your 'daddy'"—mocking the word—"sometimes, so now"—putting the index finger on my chest and poking me hard—"git!" He closed the door.

My breastbone hurt. He'd jabbed me right where the tears were. I made my blurry way down the hall, down the stairs, out.

The street was so bright. And I felt dim, confused. I would walk back to one of those newsstands and get something to drink, maybe something to read. I had to fasten myself down and not think about Daddy. Did Raymond and Eddie know where he was? No, I'd better not think about them, either, or even about me, just about how to find the bus station again, how to get myself home.

fourteen

Even if I hadn't wanted something to drink, I needed to go into a newsstand to ask directions. I'd come out of the apartment building all turned around. It was good to get inside a little space anyway. It was good to smell the sharpness of the magazines and the fuzziness of the newsprint, the tanginess of gum. I bought some. Clove. It was like the Russian tea Aunt Joy makes at Christmas.

"Say hey!" the skinny woman at the register said. "That gum all you got?" I nodded. "Five cents, then," she said. "You're one big spender." She smiled as she said this. I remembered I wanted a Coke.

"Oh, wait," I said. "I need something to drink."

"Right there," she said, motioning toward a cooler.

I came back with a cold green bottle. "Make it a

dime," she said. Her face sort of glowed, and I saw she wasn't skinny, just slim.

"Could you tell me how to get to the bus station?" I asked, holding out a dime.

"I see, I see," she said, laughing, and her laugh was like seashells rattling in a box. "You're saving up for the road."

Part of me just wanted the directions, but another part felt the fingers of her voice loosen a knot I'd been in ever since I'd found that letter. Though I couldn't have said so, I could feel that her teasing meant there were doors I didn't even see yet. Doors that led to laughing like that, to promises. Doors that just kept opening.

"Yes, ma'am," I said. "I'm a poor wayfaring stranger."

She handed me the gum, dropped my dime in the register drawer, and said, "Go left out the door and after two blocks, left again. That's your street. Follow it about ten blocks and you'll see the station on the right."

"Thanks," I said.

She put her hands on her narrow hips. The pink of her dress was like . . . what? Oh yes, peaches. Peaches. I was calling her Peaches in my mind when she said, "May not get you to 'that bright land,' but it'll sure enough get you to Greyhound."

A man was standing behind me so close his newspaper was ruffling against my neck. "Thanks again," I said, not wanting to leave. The man cleared his throat.

In a flash I'd walked those blocks and was back in that waiting room, with its colorless walls and gray-speckled floor, its ticket window and bulletin board and plastic chairs bolted together like men on a chain gang. I sat down. I'd gone to all that trouble for nothing. Unless you count the trouble I was in.

fifteen

Riding home on the bus, I did not think. I couldn't see any point in it. If a storm's coming, it's coming. You take shelter if you can but I didn't have any, since I had caused the storm in the first place. I would just get there and see what happened. I would just hear what I had to say. Even spells weren't ruled out. If one came on, I wouldn't fight it. This was the New Sonny, who'd been to Mobile and not found his daddy.

But it's hard not to think, especially with so much behind and ahead of you. Raymond and Eddie and Peaches, whose name was something else really, the Y, Mobile Bay, and then Mama—how she was going to steam up and cry or spit words or both—and the uncles, because she would haul them in for sure.

Well, if it came to it, didn't Grandpa leave the farm once and run off to Jackson? Engaged to be married and he upped and left for two weeks without telling a soul of his whereabouts. Had to sow some wild oats. That's how Grandma tells it, I think. I never listened that hard.

Whereabouts. Whereabouts unknown. I will tell them what my whereabouts were. But why I went—my . . . my *whybecause*—is something else again. Maybe nobody knows your whybecause but you. . . . This is the kind of thing that happens in your head when you're not thinking.

It was hot in that bus. It felt crowded, even though it wasn't. Old women who carried shopping bags shaped like them, a mother and daughter all dressed up except the little girl had a skate key on a dirty string around her neck, a scrawny boy, older than me, jumpy, who kept looking around at everybody like we were dangerous, a young colored man in the back with a book.

Outside the window, fields of cotton and peanuts stretched out like that was all there was in the world—no cities packed with people who were not your daddy, no small towns where furious mamas lay in wait.

We drove out of that, though, and smack into Andalusia. I went slowly down the big bus steps, then ran to the trees across the road, scared my bike would be somebody else's by now. Whew! There it was. I hopped on and pedaled hard, like I WANTED to get home, which I did by now, because even with not thinking I had got to that smothery place where you just want the storm to hit and get it over with.

Coasting into Mozier, I thought how it was just a little place: a few streets, a spot, and my family and me, we were flecks, and—oh forget it, Sonny, I said to myself, turning into the driveway at our house on Rhubarb. Wait'll your mama shows you what a fleck can do.

But Mama wasn't there. "I'm home!" I hollered as I came in the back door.

"Well, don't bust our eardrums about it," Loretta said from the kitchen table, where she and Deaton appeared to be eating graham crackers and milk for supper. Cantaloupe was lapping milk from a saucer by Deaton's chair. "I *told* Mama we'd never get rid of you that easy."

"Where *is* Mama?" I asked.

"At the *hospital*," Deaton answered.

My heart jumped. "What happened?"

"Oh, Mama's fine, Sonny, except you took ten years off of her life by running away. She had the police out and everything. It's one of Mamby's kids who's in the doctors' clutches."

"She might DIE," Deaton said. His eyes wide, his eyeballs the same marbly white as the milk in his bowl.

"So where've you been?" Loretta asked.

"Give me a minute," I said. I walked down the hall to

the living room. Everything was just like I'd left it yesterday morning—the rose-colored couch and blue chairs, the coffee table reddish gold in the late light—only it was sort of shrunk. I stopped by the bathroom. Looking in the mirror, I saw I was the same except for my eyes—

"Sonny!"

"Mobile," I said. Back in the kitchen I took some graham crackers out of the paper pack on the table and got a bowl to break them up in. "I took the bus from Andalusia."

"Why?" Deaton asked.

"To see what's there," I told him.

"I don't believe you," Loretta said.

"Why?" Deaton asked.

"Because he's lying," Loretta said. "Sonny's about as adventuresome as moss."

I hadn't even poured the milk on when we heard the gravel crunch as a car pulled into the driveway.

"Get ready for the show," Loretta said, grinning. "Last words, Sonny? Or"—she slid a ribbon of paper across the table to me—"do you want to leave another helpful note?"

I was about to make some smart remark—though never as smart as Loretta's—when I heard not one but *two* car doors slam. Oh Lord, let it be Uncle Hickman or Uncle Marty. If it's got to be a man with Mama, don't let it be Uncle Sink.

"Sonny!" Mama shrieked when she saw me through the screen door. "Sonny, you're home!" She rushed in and I stood up and she grabbed me to her and gave me a rib-crushing hug. "Oh Sonny, oh my boy," she kept saying. Then she held me at arm's length. "Let me look at you." Past her, I could see Uncle Sink in the doorway, blocking the light.

"Ooooohhh, Sonny!" Loretta trilled. "Home from the wars . . ."

Mama dropped her hands and looked at Loretta. "If you'd seen what I've just seen," she said. "If you'd seen Nissa—"

"Where have you been, boy?" Uncle Sink demanded.

"But I don't know, Loretta," Mama went on. "I don't know what your heart's made of." There were tears all down Mama's face and on my shirt where she'd hugged me. Her yellow dress was crushed and wilted.

"Muscle," Loretta said. "Thank God."

"Answer me, Sonny." That was Uncle Sink.

"Mobile," I said.

"Mobile what?" he barked.

"Alabama?" Deaton asked.

Loretta hooted.

"Mobile, *sir*," I said.

"Whatever made you—," Mama started.

"Doing what?" Uncle Sink cut in.

I froze. Uncle Sink's hands were fists and his cheek was twitching. I took a deep breath. Then I saw one little way I might save my skin, and I took it.

"Seeing a little of the world, sir. Sowing wild oats."

"Like he had any!" Loretta said.

Uncle Sink wrestled a smile and won. "Come on outside, Sonny."

"Sinclair . . . ," Mama said.

He looked at her. Raised his red woolly-worm eyebrows. "A man's got to take what's coming to him, Selma."

Mama nodded, then gave me a sharp look. "The police were out hunting for you all night. Sinclair and Hickman and Marty, too," she said angrily, then called, "Don't hurt him!" as I followed Uncle Sink out the door.

sixteen

In another year, two at the most, I'd be big as Uncle Sink and he wouldn't be able to get away with this. He took off his belt as he walked. I followed, watching it whip through the back loops of his work pants and disappear in front of him like a snake around a rock. We went behind the garage like always so we were hidden from the kitchen windows and the neighbors. The smell of pine needles and motor oil is stapled in my mind to the *thwack* of that belt across my backside and the pain like fire with a knife in it.

Facing the back wall, I put my hands on the unpainted wood over my head and leaned forward. The belt came down, and I gave a little *uhh.* I was allowed that. No crying. And no bleeding, Uncle Sink said, as if I could help it.

After he'd hit me eight times, he said, between lashes,

"You're"—*Whap!*—"thirteen."—*Whap!*—"I'll give"—*Whap!*—"you that."—*Whap!*—"And one"—*Whap!*—"to grow on!"—*Whap!*

When he'd finished, my legs and hands were trembling as I turned back to face him. At least he didn't make me take my pants down. That was the one good thing.

"Sonny," he said, gliding his whip back into its groove and buckling it on, "you might as well be my boy, for all the daddy you got in this world, so I've got to say to you what I say to Albion."

Sour juice rose in my mouth. I nodded.

"That's a wild man you got down there." He gestured to my crotch. "Keep him zipped as much as you can, and when you can't, keep him clean."

"Yes, sir," I said.

"And don't EVER run off like that again! Your mother can only take so much."

"Yes, sir."

"Don't forget this family's full of bad hearts."

"No, sir."

My legs were plain shaking by then. I needed to lie down. "Could we go in?" I asked.

Uncle Sink put his hands on my shoulders, grasping the bones like they were pipes he was fixing to fit and solder together. "Takes character to be a man," he said. "You need to know anything, you ask me."

"Yes, sir." My voice was getting wobbly too. I knew I was supposed to say thank you. Thank you for doing your duty, Uncle Sink. Thank you for hitting me. For hating me. Thank you for thinking I'm just like you.

"Don't drop on me, soldier!" he ordered. "Get in the house."

So I walked the short way to the back stoop, up the steps, through the kitchen, full of voices and eyes, and down the little hall to my room. I lay on my stomach on the navy blue bedspread and stretched my arms out like wings. I'd be an airplane now. Pain—well, that was just combustion in the engine, propeller blades slicing up the air.

seventeen

That airplane didn't land till morning, which is when I found out about Nissa. She's Mamby's oldest child, seventeen like Loretta. And she has a boyfriend already out of school named Freelan Diggs. He took her fishing on Thursday, the day before I left, and somehow she stepped on a fish-hook in the bottom of the boat.

On Friday morning her foot was puffy and by that after-noon she was feeling sick. By Saturday morning it was her whole leg that had swelled and she was real bad off by the time they got her to the hospital. So Mama had gone over to see her when she got off work. On Sunday she wanted to go again and she wanted me to go with her. Her plan was for Loretta to keep Deaton, but Loretta was nowhere to be found, so Mama asked Mrs. Jackson next door.

"A pleasure," Mrs. Jackson said, holding the screen door open for Deaton to come in. "Deaton's the best-behaved boy in Mozier." I don't know where she got that. "Glad to see *you're* back," she added, looking at me.

Mama smiled and thanked her, then said angrily as we turned away and walked toward the car, "Sinclair says not to ask you any questions. 'Boys will be boys,' he says. But I want you to promise me that you'll never, NEVER take off like that again."

"I promise," I said, then got in the car.

Behind the steering wheel, Mama went on like she didn't hear. "It's bad enough what this world can *do* to your children—look at Nissa—in an *instant*, Sonny, in the batting of an eye when they're right beside you. But to think that you would run off to Mobile, offer yourself as bait to the horrors of this world—"

"Mama—"

"I'm not finished!" She put the key in the ignition. "You don't know a thing about life! What it takes to birth it, feed it, protect it. You have no right to throw yourself away! You hear me? No *right*!"

Shaking with anger and blurry-eyed with tears, Mama turned the key. The Buick hesitated a second and then rumbled, ready to go.

"I'm sorry," I said.

"You ought to be," she told me.

I'd only been in the Andalusia Hospital once, and that was when Grandpa had an operation right before he died. His room was on the third floor, where everything was hushed and clean and quiet. It didn't occur to me that Mamby's girl wouldn't be in the same sort of place.

But the colored part of the hospital was in the basement. It was damp and the old cream-coffee-colored paint was flaking. Also, instead of sharing a room with one other person like Grandpa had, Nissa was in what Mama called a ward, with five beds lined up on either side of a long narrow room.

It didn't look exactly clean, either, but it was hard to tell because it was so dingy and run-down. And it smelled bad. I wanted to turn tail and run as soon as we got there, but Mama walked straight toward Mamby, and I followed.

Mamby was seated, her big body balanced on a stool, which was all that would fit between the beds. She had her face turned up and her eyes closed, and she was holding her daughter's hand. Nissa, skinny and lighter than Mamby, lay straight as an arrow between worn-out sheets. One of the legs under the covers was big as a stovepipe. I stole a look at her face. It was bathed in sweat, her eyes fixed on the ceiling.

Mama hesitated just a minute at the end of the bed, then walked over, leaned down, and put her arms around

Mamby. I'd seen Mama go to Mamby for comfort when Daddy left and when Grandpa died upstairs in this same building, but this was the first time I'd seen Mama give comfort back.

Mamby made a low moan. "They gonna take it off," she said. "My baby's leg. At the knee."

"Oh no, Verna," Mama said. "I'm so sorry." She stood up. Mamby's name was Verna?

Nissa turned her head back and forth on the pillow, and Mamby leaned toward her. "She's got the sugar, my baby has, and that fishhook done poisoned her blood before her and Freelan even got home with the fish."

"Freelan must feel terrible," Mama said.

Mamby nodded. "Heartbroke. He wanted to marry this girl."

"He still will, won't he?" I said, though I didn't mean to say anything.

"Sonny!" Mamby called out, a flicker of light in her voice. "Come here to me." I did, and she hugged me tight. "I didn't see you, child. I didn't know you was here." She let me go and took up Nissa's hand again. "I don't know," she said. "Nobody knows but the Lord."

"What can we do, Verna?" Mama asked. "Can I take food to your other children?"

"No, honey, no," Mamby said. "My sister Sofia, she's feeding them. Looking after them, too. Mr. Bill's gone on the Chicago run. Lord, Lord," she finished, almost under her breath.

Mr. Bill's Mamby's husband. He works for the railroad.

"Have you had any supper?" Mama asked.

"Haven't wanted any."

"You've got to keep up your strength," Mama said. "How about Sonny and I sit with Nissa, and you go home and get some rest?"

Mamby looked at Mama hard. "You wouldn't leave *him,* Selma," she said.

"No," Mama admitted.

"I'm no different."

"Of course, of course," Mama said, and I thought she was going to cry. "I'll go home and fix some sandwiches and a thermos of coffee and send them back by Sonny. Then when you *can* eat, you'll have something here."

"I'd welcome coffee. I would," Mamby said.

"We'll do it, then," Mama told her. "If you think of something else, just tell Sonny." She turned toward me as if we were leaving, then turned back toward Mamby. "And Verna," she said, her voice uncertain, "Joy and Roo and I, we'll make up some money. . . ."

Mamby lifted her head. She could have been accepting, could have been pulling away. "You all go on now," she said.

eighteen

I did take Mamby dinner that night—ham salad sandwiches and Dolly Madison coconut cake, along with the coffee— but the next day was Nissa's operation, so Mama went to the hospital by herself after work. Before she left, she collared Loretta to make a meat loaf, and Deaton and I went in the kitchen to watch. Loretta hates being watched.

First she nicked her thumb chopping onions, then when she cracked an egg on the rim of the mixing bowl, half the shell went in and all the egg went out.

"Get out of here!" she yelled, but we didn't budge.

When Loretta gets mad, her face takes on a bricky look and her freckles poke right through whatever goop she's put on her face. It's something. She broke another egg. "I don't see why I have to cook dinner just because Mamby's kid is in the hospital," she said, one hand up to the wrist in hamburger, egg, and onion.

"What about us?" I said. "*We* have to eat it."

She shook her beef-flecked fist at me. Cornflakes from breakfast were scattered at my end of the table and I flicked one at Deaton, but he didn't notice.

"How do they take your leg off?" he asked. "Can they unhook it?"

"I don't think so," I said. That was just what I was hoping he wouldn't ask. Deaton still gets nightmares.

"With a saw," Loretta told him, scooping the ball of meat into a loaf pan.

"A *saw?*" Deaton's mouth hung open and his gray eyes looked big as nickels.

"Retta, can't you—," I started.

She wheeled around. "What? Can't I LIE, like everyone else in this chloroformed family? No, I can't. And it wouldn't help precious Deaton here if I did. I could say the doctors charm legs off, but somebody in the operating room would still be sharpening the saw."

"Ooooooh!" Deaton squealed, color coming back to his face.

"Life is full of poison fishhooks and cut-off legs, and there's no future in pretending otherwise."

The oven door gave a springy creak as Loretta opened it and slid the meat loaf in. I could see potatoes already on the rack. She walked to the sink to wash her hands. "Speaking of lies, Sonny," she said over the rush of tap water, "where the hell *were* you Friday night and Saturday?" She turned to face me, drying her hands on a dish towel.

I didn't say anything.

"*Hey!* Leon Junior!" she cried in a cranky-teacher voice, "I'm talking to you."

"Your name is Leon?" Deaton asked.

"Yeah," I said. "They called me Sonny when Daddy was here so as not to get us confused."

"And they call you Sonny now because nobody wants to say *Leon*." Loretta yanked open the Frigidaire door. "Leon! Leon! Leon!" she taunted, grabbing lettuce and then carrots from the crisper and throwing them over her shoulder. I caught them. "Good," she said, when she straightened up and turned around. "You make the salad."

"Tossed, I guess," I said.

Loretta didn't even smile at this, but all Deaton's shock over the saw went into giggles and he laughed till he got the hiccups.

"Plug yourself up," Loretta said to him, holding out a blob of half-baked dough she'd pinched off the brown-and-serve rolls. She opened the cupboard and scooted cans around till she found one she wanted, then cranked it open and dumped peas into a saucepan. *"Sonny,"* she said, "Where *were* you?"

"You heard me tell Mama—I took a bus to Mobile and spent the night at the YMCA."

"Oh, I see," Loretta said, back at the Frigidaire, rooting in the compartments on the door. "We don't have any butter. Deaton, you go next door and borrow some."

"But Retta—"

"Mrs. Jackson loves you. Go on."

"That's the trouble," Deaton whined. "She pets my head."

"The suffering!" Loretta mocked. "Do you want dry rolls, Deaton?" He shook his head. "Naked potatoes?"

"No."

"So scram!" He ran out the back door.

Her green eyes drilled into me. "Let's have it, Sonny Boy."

I stood up. "Talking to you is like going to the dentist," I said.

"Thanks."

I didn't know I wasn't going to tell her till then. "I told you," I said.

"You did not! Even assuming you did go to Mobile, you never said why or what you did there. You can't fool me like you can Mama."

"I looked around," I said.

Loretta came at me, hands raised, ready to shake me by the shoulders like she did when I was smaller, but I put the heel of my hand on her forehead and stepped back, straightening my arm. She could throw her fists out all she wanted, but she couldn't reach me. This infuriated her. She was going for the pancake turner on the counter when we heard the front door open. Truce.

Mama came through the living room and dining room and into the kitchen. She looked at us, her face paper-white.

"That poor soul," she said. "That poor, poor soul."

Deaton bounded in the back door. "All she had was this," he said, holding out a stick of margarine.

Loretta took it and looked at Mama. "So much for living in one of the butter neighborhoods."

nineteen

Nissa came through the surgery fine, but she had to be in the hospital for a while. Mamby stayed with her round the clock to begin with. Then she had to start working again.

The first day back at our house, Mamby was going to fix Swiss steak for supper and asked Mama if she could take a plate to Nissa. "She's lost a lot more than they cut off," Mamby said. "She's lost her taste for this world. And all they serve up over there is slop."

"Take whatever you think she needs," Mama said as she left for work.

So around five o'clock Mamby had steak and mashed potatoes, green beans and fried apples, all fixed on a plate and covered with foil, and was about to leave when the phone rang and it was Aunt Roo saying a neighbor of

Mamby's sister Sofia had run over to tell her Sofia had hurt her back and needed Mamby's help right away.

"Sofia's too old for babies, and right now she's got mine, too," Mamby told me when she hung up. "No wonder her back went out."

I started to ask how many Sofia had, but Mamby held out the plate. "Could you take this to Nissa for me, Sonny? It'll be cold by the time I can get there." I must have looked unsure. "Don't you worry," she told me. "The nurses will let you in."

So that's how I wound up taking Nissa her dinner. The nurses weren't what I was worried about. I hoped Nissa would be asleep when I got there, so I could put the plate down and run, but she wasn't. The other three patients on the ward seemed to be asleep, though. One old man was curled up like a baby, with his pillow in his arms. Walking over to Nissa's bed, I was careful just to look at her face, but it didn't matter. I could feel the pit where her leg had been.

"Nissa," I said, holding out the offering. "Mamby—I mean, Verna—your *mama* sent you this."

She was flat on her back, not propped up in bed, so she didn't reach for it. She just looked at me, her dark eyes hazy, like chocolate drops.

"I'm Sonny Bradshaw," I told her, as if that meant anything.

"Thanks," she said.

That was my chance to leave. I'll never know why I didn't. Instead, I crimped the silver foil tighter around the plate and set it on the bedside table. Then I pulled up a stool and sat down.

Nissa turned her eyes to me. They were more focused.

"It's awful about your leg," I said. "It's not fair."

She looked at me harder. There was such emptiness where her leg had been, I had to keep talking.

"But your whole life . . ." I was slow with these words, as if I had to take each one out of a box and unwrap it. ". . . it's still there. It's not cut off." The *wrong words,* I said to myself. The *worst* words. I went on. "Your boyfriend, he still loves you—"

"What're you *talking* about?" Nissa asked. There was a sort of purr in her voice. She was lots older than me and she was a girl and she was . . .

"I don't know," I said.

Nissa's face brightened, and she gave a little hoot of laughter. "That's the truthfullest thing I've heard since I got here," she said.

"But I—"

"Everybody in this hospital, everybody in this *town* knows, Sonny Bradshaw. They know and they're every one telling me. Even my mama. What did you call her— Mamby? Lord help us, Miss Scarlett! Even my mama has got the shoes of wisdom on her feet. Not a soul sees it's a different world with only one foot to stand on. Nobody but this idiot white boy. You *know* you don't know, Sonny. That's something."

I just looked at her. I felt like I'd been slapped on one cheek and kissed on the other. "It's Swiss steak," I said, pointing to the plate. "You should eat some while it's hot."

Where were these words coming from?

"Oh, give it here," Nissa said, putting her hands palm down at her sides and squirming into a sitting position. Her face knotted up for a minute, and her pillow was now half off the bed.

"I could fix that for you," I said, feeling all at once like I couldn't come an inch closer to her to save my life.

"Thanks," she said again.

My legs were wobbly, my arms were too long, and my fingers seemed to bend in all directions, but somehow I got over to the bed, leaned down, put my arms around Nissa, and scooted the pillow slantways against the wall. I had to touch her hot back doing this. Oh, God.

Then I took the foil off the plate and handed it to her, along with silverware rolled up in a blue napkin. Mamby had cut the steak up. She knew there were no tables for the basement beds.

Nissa took a bite of potatoes, closed her eyes a minute, then opened them again and said, "So what are you up to, Sonny?"

Did she know I'd been gone? "What do you mean?" I asked.

"Everybody's up to something," she said. "I was up to courting when I got hooked."

"I ran away," I told her, then sat there, stunned. What did I say that for?

"Where to?" she asked between bites of steak.

"You're eating," I said.

"You brought me food."

"But your mama said—" Then I thought maybe I shouldn't repeat that. So part of my brain *was* working. . . .

"This is my favorite," Nissa explained. "Where'd you go?"

I leaned over and whispered, "I went to Mobile, but listen, Nissa. Don't tell anybody why. I went looking for my daddy."

"He skedaddle?" she asked too loud.

"When I was little," I said.

"You find him?"

I nodded.

"You see any water around here?" she asked.

I found a plastic pitcher and a glass on the windowsill above the bedside table. The window was set in a well at ground level, so it looked out on roots and weeds. I poured Nissa some water and she rested her fork on her plate to take it. She drained the glass and handed it back.

"So what was *he* up to?"

Nissa was the funniest girl I'd ever met. She seemed to be interested in the *story*, not who was right or who was wrong. I didn't know what to make of her.

"I don't know," I said.

She gave that laugh again. "I just about like you," she told me. "Can't eat any more food, though." She laid her silverware on the plate, spread the napkin over it, and held it up to me. I took it, pretty sure she was through talking, too.

"You won't—," I started. She was scooting back down in the bed again. I stood up and moved the pillow for her, then backed away.

"No, no," she said. "Don't worry. Pretty soon I'll have a hollow leg to keep all my secrets in."

That made me kind of sick.

"I'm kidding," she said softly.

"I know."

"That's something, then." She closed her eyes. "Thanks for dinner."

"Your mama's coming later." I'd almost forgot to tell her. "She had to go to Sofia's because . . ."

But Nissa was asleep.

twenty

Talking to Nissa got me really confused. First there was feeling like I'd lost something when I left the hospital. But I figured I was just shook up from seeing a young person in that kind of fix. Then later in the evening, I tried to go back to our talk in my mind. It wasn't finished somehow, but I didn't know what to do with it. So I went to bed, only to fall asleep and wake up, fall asleep and wake up.

The next morning I felt, as Mamby—I mean, Verna—says, "like the hind end of bad luck." But I had to go to work, so I got myself ready and over to the Circle of Life on time. I couldn't pay attention, though. Uncle Marty kept having to tell me things two and three times. When I made no move after the third time he told me to fill out the supply order sheet, he said, "Sonny, are you sick?"

"No sir," I said.

"Are you moping about something?"

I shook my head. "I was up late," I lied, "listening to *Texaco Playhouse*." That's one of Loretta's shows—stupid, stupid—and anybody who knew me would know I'd never sit still for it.

"Well, here," he said, reaching for the coffeepot with one hand and a paper cup with the other. "Drink this and see if you can come to your senses."

I tried. I put in enough sugar cubes to make the spoon stand up, plus whitening it good with the milk. But it still tasted like hot water you'd soaked a leather belt in.

Uncle Marty handed me a pencil and I started filling out the order, saying to myself:

five hundred pounds of white flour
one hundred pounds of fry shortening
two hundred pounds of plain sugar
a hundred pounds of confectioners'

and on and on as I filled in the lines, trying to focus my mind.

But my mind was back at the hospital, collecting everything Nissa had said and done so I could bring it to the workroom at the Circle of Life. What did "I just about like you" mean? What about the way she laughed? What about the damp heat of her back that I hadn't meant to touch? What about her being there at all, Mamby's daughter, there with *me*, and that awful emptiness that had been the calf of her leg, her ankle, her foot? Why was I thinking like this?

"*Sonny!*" Uncle Marty called out—not for the first time, I could tell. "Ramey is here. Are you done?"

I was, I thought. I read down the form: flour, lard, sugars, eggs, milk, chocolate, cinnamon, yeast. "I think so," I told him, handing it over.

Uncle Marty's eyes zigzagged down the page. "Lord have mercy, Sonny," he said. "There's no meat on here. No potatoes or onions or lettuce—nothing but donut makings." He turned to Ramey, the driver for Whitney's Wholesale Foods. "Excuse me," he said. "This boy's head's come loose today. I'll have the order for you in a minute. Sonny," he said to me, "get Ramey some coffee and an éclair."

"No, no éclair," Ramey said, pulling his head back against the collar of his blue jumpsuit and showing his double chin. "Just the coffee, Sonny. That sweetness is too much for me."

I got him a mug, bone white, thick as a wrist, and I watched the coffee go in, acorn brown.

"A little milk," he told me, so I tipped that in, white disappearing into brown.

And in my head, in the cup of the day, his words and Nissa's swirled: "I just about like you." Coffee and cream. "That sweetness is too much for me."

twenty-one

I was hoping Mama would go back to see Nissa and ask me to go with her, but she didn't. Once it looked like Nissa was doing okay, Mama slid back over the line. The line you can't see that cuts off Mamby and Nissa's life from ours. Mamby crosses the line to come here, but maybe it's okay to cross in that direction. Or maybe it's because she gets paid.

I tried to ask Mama about this, after supper one night, but I got nowhere. The kitchen was all cleaned up— Loretta had scoured the skin off the dishes—and Mama was sitting at the table with a stack of green stamps, two books to paste them in, and a bowl with a little water and a sponge in it. She'd open the book to a blank page, flatten it with the heel of her hand, then lay a block of stamps on the sponge and peck at it with her fingers to get it wet. I would have licked it myself.

"Mama," I said, standing at the far end of the gray-and-yellow dinette set, "why is it that Mamby comes here but we never go to her house?"

Mama looked up from her task of positioning stamps within the big rectangle on the page. She raised her drawn-on eyebrows. "Mamby is our *employee*," she said, pronouncing the word as if she held it out far in front of her. Then, in case that wasn't enough, she added, "I'm Mr. Boykin's employee and we don't go to his house."

"But you work in his *store*," I said. "That's different. You don't know his family—"

"I've known Mabel Boykin since I was a girl," she said. "She was our church organist."

"But she didn't fix your food and. . . ." And hug your children, I wanted to say, but for some reason I didn't.

"Sonny," Mama said, "you're making me tired."

"I'm sorry," I said. But halfway down the "sorry" hill, my feelings picked up speed and rolled right into mad. You just *give up* is your problem, I wanted to say to Mama. You don't have any gumption.

"Gumption" is Grandpa's word. "God gave us talents, Sonny," he used to say. "They're our tools. But the handle of every tool is gumption."

Once I got Grandpa out of my head, I had to admit

Mama did have gumption. Why else was she saving stamps for stuff we didn't have money for? She was holding the family together with a cereal bowl and a sponge.

"Can I ask you something else?" I said.

"Ask away."

"Who's Miss Scarlett?"

"In Mozier?" Mama asked. She'd run out of big blocks of stamps now and was piecing double rows and even single stamps on a page.

"I don't know. It's what Nissa said about us calling Mamby 'Mamby.' She said, 'Lord help us, Miss Scarlett.'"

"Oh," Mama said. "That's Scarlett O'Hara."

"Who's she?"

"A character in *Gone with the Wind*."

"What's that?"

"A movie," Mama said. "Well, it was a book first. I wasn't much older than you when I saw it."

"What's it about?"

"The Civil War," she said. "And hard times after." She had pasted the last stamp down and was stacking the books and putting the rubber band back on. "That's fourteen," she said. "Two more and we get a floor lamp."

"What's the Civil War got to do with Mamby?" I asked, and then said, "Oh. Oh, I see." I didn't so much see as feel. Sort of sick. "Is Miss Scarlett colored?"

Loretta appeared in the doorway. She'd got the front

part of her hair put on top of her head and she looked almost soft. Then she spoke. "'Is Miss Scarlett colored?' Sonny, we ought to keep you in a closet. Miss Scarlett is 'the flower of Southern womanhood watered by the sweat and tears of slaves.'"

"You hush your mouth, Loretta Bradshaw!" Mama hissed. I was shocked. She lets Loretta say *anything*.

"I'm just saying what I saw in the movie and read in the book," Loretta insisted.

"You better watch yourself," Mama warned.

"Why?" I asked.

"And you too," Mama said. "There's colored and there's white in this town and everywhere else. Mamby is a good and decent woman, but she has her kind and we have ours and that's the way God wanted it."

That's not the way *I* want it, I thought. And her name is *not* Mamby.

twenty-two

"See you later," Loretta called from the doorway. "Wesley and I are going to get a milk shake."

"Wesley?" Mama said, like it was hardly even a word. "Wesley who?"

Loretta touched her fingertips to her forehead, then flung her hand out in exasperation. "Wes-ley Row-lett," she said, as if Mama had gone dim.

"Will Rowlett's boy?" she asked, standing up now, the stamp books clutched to her chest.

"The selfsame," Loretta said, with that down-the-nose look that more than once had earned her a slap.

"He's no good, Loretta," Mama declared. "He's known for shady dealings."

"That's not Wesley's fault," Loretta said. "You can't

blame boys for no-account daddies, and anyway, at least *his* daddy is here."

Mama's rounded back went straight and stiff. She yanked the junk drawer open, slapped the stamp books inside, and closed it with a bang. "I'd be ashamed of myself, Loretta Bradshaw," she said.

"Well, *I'm* not," Loretta shot back, and clomped down the hall. Loretta can't weigh much but she sure can make noise. I followed her.

We were all the way out on the porch before I spoke.

"Does Wesley have a car?" I asked, startling Loretta so much that she took one step too many and lurched off into the yard.

"No, Sonny," she said. "He's coming in a surrey with a fringe on top."

"What's that?"

"You groundhog! It's a buggy. Pulled by a horsey."

I ignored her. "Do you know Verna's last name?" I asked.

"Verna?"

"Mamby, *you* groundhog."

A smile hovered on her lips but she bit it off. "Peak, I think. Or Preece."

"Where does she live?"

"Sonny, were you born in a bucket? She lives out Staniford Road like all the colored people in this town."

Verna Preece. Staniford Road. Nissa. Nissa Peak. Nissa Preece. It had to be "Preece"—that sounded so good with "Nissa."

"Bye, Blind Boy!" Loretta called, climbing on the back of—good Lord, Wesley had a motorcycle! Mama would have a conniption. "You tell her and I'll pinch your head off!" Loretta yelled. Then Wesley rolled the handlebar throttle and they roared away.

I expected Mama to come charging out the front door at that sound, but she didn't. When I went back in, she was still in the kitchen folding sheets and listening to Deaton's explanation of how Cantaloupe got in the Frigidaire. "She must have jumped in after the tuna salad," Deaton said, squashing the towel-swaddled ball of orange fur in his arms.

"Well, she about gave me a heart attack," Mama said, pulling me into the conversation with her eyes. "I open the door to get a drink of ice water and . . ." Mama holds her hand out palm up as if she were giving us something. And all of a sudden I see she's not mad at Deaton. Or Cantaloupe. She's upset about Loretta going off wherever she takes a notion. And she's trying to make us laugh so we won't see it.

A voice in the back of my head says, Mama's not in control and she knows it, and I start to feel sick like somebody took a hammer to my shin. My spit tastes like wire.

I look hard at Deaton, at Cantaloupe, but I can't hold them. They start to blur and waver, and far off, a bird squawks "Sonny!" just as the lights go out.

"Get that cat out of here!" Mama was ordering Deaton as I cracked my eyes. "Oh, Sonny," she said, mopping my face with a wet washrag, "I thought we were done with this."

I tried to say, "Me too," but the words rolled around like a bunch of grapes in my mouth. I made an ugly sound.

"Hush," Mama said. "You'll scare Deaton."

So I had to lie there silent on the kitchen floor with evening like a . . . like a calendar page flopping at the window—Grandpa's *Farmer's Almanac* calendar, which is why he and Uncle Sink were heaving me up off the linoleum and onto the couch.

"You call Burton?" Grandpa asked, even though he was dead and Burton was the doctor who hadn't been able to save him. "That's a bad lick on his forehead."

It's just a kitten, I thought, just Cantaloupe licking me. Old Frozen Fur, washing my face.

"Look at his eyes, Selma," Uncle Sink said. "He don't look like himself."

"He looks like Leon when I hit him with that dinner tray," Mama said.

"What?" That was Grandpa and Uncle Sink and Deaton. "What? What?"

Whoa, Mama! My mind went around a curve and there was my voice. "She threw his dinner at him," I said, my words just a little slushy. "The night before he left. She let him have it."

"Never miss a thing, do you, Son?" Mama said.

I miss Daddy, I thought. "No, ma'am."

"Well, keep it to yourself," the voice that had been Grandpa's but was now Uncle Hickman's said. "There are some things a man would rather not know."

twenty-three

Dr. Burton said I should stay awake for eight hours. I had whacked my head twice going down—first on the table and then on the floor—and he wanted to be sure I didn't go unconscious. Mama explained this to Loretta when she sauntered in long past dark. "Could we tell?" Loretta asked.

"You have no room to talk, young lady," Mama said. "You appear to have lost what wits you were given."

"Thanks," Loretta said.

"I just hope that's all you've lost."

"Selma!" Loretta said, faking shock. "Not in front of the children."

"I don't have to take this!" Mama spat back. "Go to your room!" And Loretta carried herself out like a queen.

I looked at Mama sitting in what she called "Mertie's

little wingback" because it had belonged to her sister who had died. She looked blurry and halfway collapsed.

"You have to go to work in the morning?" I asked her.

"Does the sun have to come up?" she asked. "Does the boll weevil have to eat cotton?"

"You sound like Loretta!" I said. "Why don't you get her to sit with me so you can go to sleep?"

"After she stayed out till? . . ." Mama started, but the same thought that hit me must have hit her.

"Loretta *loves* her sleep," I said.

Mama looked at me like I was a bulb that had just got brighter. "I'll do it," she said.

After thirty minutes of wrangling and Mama's saying a threatening "Good night" to both of us, Loretta was sitting in the little wingback with a newspaper in her lap.

"What a brother," she said. "Just the pea brain I want to stay up all night with."

"But Mama looks like a dishrag, Loretta, and she's got to go to work in the morning."

"Oh, poor Mama," Loretta warbled. "Poor Saint Selma . . ."

I wanted to tell her about what started my spell, about seeing Mama scared and trying to hide it after Loretta had walked out. I was fishing around for the words when Loretta hit me in the face with the newspaper. "Don't close your eyes!" she hissed.

I was sitting at one end of the couch, nothing but the end table with the vase lamp on it between me and Loretta in her chair, and my eyes shot open just in time to see my arm sweep across the table, knock over the lamp, and smack Loretta in the ear.

"Jesus in a jumpsuit!" Loretta yelped, leaping up to catch the vase before it hit the floor. "Are you crazy, Sonny?"

"Nobody likes to be hit in the face," I told her.

She leaned down to pick up the newspaper she had hit me with. Two magazines slid out. Ahhhhh! Retta's secret reading.

"What have you got here?" I asked, amazed that Loretta hid anything.

She held them up: *True Confessions* and *Popular Mechanics.* And Mama thinks *I'm* weird.

"Why do you have *that?*" I asked, pointing to a cover boasting glorified engine parts.

"Wesley's teaching me to work on his motorcycle," she said.

"And the other one?"

"I'm looking for lines," she said.

"You're in a play?"

"Every day of this world. You too, little Leon. After supper you played the scene where you have the fit."

"It wasn't a *fit,*" I said. "It was—"

"The spell, then. And now—"

"Retta, I found out tonight that these spells are ABOUT something," I declared.

"Faulty wiring," she said.

"No."

"Carbon buildup on the pistons."

"I mean they happen because I *see* something."

"Yeah? Well, so do the folks who drop and roll at One-Way," Loretta reminded me.

"I don't mean *visions*, Retta. I mean I see how things *are*. Tonight I saw that Mama—"

"Drinks," Loretta cut in.

"Drinks?" My voice went higher and too loud.

"Oh, yes," said Loretta Wise-Woman. "That Get-Set bottle on her dresser is really full of gin."

"I don't believe that!"

"It's a free country," Retta said. "But next time you're here and Mama's not, why don't you spray a little Get-Set in your hand. See if it gives *you* style."

I sat there, staring at "the little cherry drop leaf," as Mama calls the coffee table.

"She makes it all miniature," I said.

"Don't DO that!" Loretta snapped.

"What?"

"Turn without a signal. Conversation is like *driving*, Sonny. If you're going to make a big move, you have to let other people know. Put on the blinker. Otherwise they lose you."

"Or run into you," I added.

"You got it," she said. "Now what the hell were you talking about?" I laughed. Loretta *can* make me feel better.

"Well, Mama calls the chair you're sitting in 'Mertie's little wingback' and that"—I touched the coffee table with my bare foot—"is her 'little cherry dropleaf' and I was just wondering if we live in Mama's miniature world."

"I think you're onto something," she said. "After all, aren't we up at this hour because of 'Sonny's little problem'?"

"Definitely," I said.

"And didn't we move to this house because of 'Leon's little absence'?"

"Nobody said that."

"Which makes it even smaller," Loretta insisted.

I nodded.

"And now Mama's got her 'little drinking.'"

"What about you, Retta? What have you got?"

Loretta did what she does that's like smiling. Then she pulled out whatever pins had organized her hair. She shook her head, and her hair stood out in red points. "Wrenches," she said. "Loretta's little wrenches."

twenty-four

When the sun was just starting to show behind the water tower, Retta said, "Well, you're still alive. Time to chop onions."

"What?" So much for conversation signals.

"I'm going to fix us scrambled eggs and hash browns."

"All *right*!" I said, standing up, then feeling woozy.

Retta looked at me. "Wet washrag," she said. "On your face first, then on the back of your neck."

"Okay," I said, and kind of swung down the hall to the bathroom. I felt like wind chimes.

Steadied by my sister's medicine, I came back to the kitchen, where three wrinkly-skin baked potatoes were on the counter, an onion was on the chopping board, and Loretta was opening the egg carton.

"Takes forever if you start with raw potatoes," she explained. "I'm glad Mamby baked extra."

"Verna," I corrected.

"Knock-knock," Loretta said as she cracked the egg on the edge of the little mixing bowl.

"Who's there?"

"Mayonnaise."

"You're going to put mayonnaise in the eggs?" Gag.

"Wrong. You're supposed to say, 'Mayonnaise who?'"

I obliged. And she sang, in her clarinet-with-a-dry-reed voice, "Mayonnaise have seen the glory . . ."

"You're changing the subject," I said. "You just don't want to call her Verna." The new Sonny wasn't going to be distracted.

Loretta lit into the eggs with a fork till they were frothy. Then she handed me a knife. "Chop-chop," she ordered.

"When you answer," I said.

"Look, Leon, you can call Mamby 'Mamby' or 'Verna' or 'Our Lady of Staniford Road' and she'll still get the hind foot of everything and live in a house you can see daylight under."

"But at least I'll be saying her real name."

"Do you call Mrs. Jackson by her first name?" Loretta asked.

I had three layers of skin off the onion and was working on a fourth. "No."

"Speed it up, Sonny. You're not painting the Sistine Chapel."

"Okay," I said, getting the last of the golden paper off but taking a layer of white flesh with it. "I could call her 'Mrs. Preece,'" I suggested.

"She'd laugh," Retta said.

"Well—"

"You don't call Aunt Roo 'Mrs. Carlisle,'" Retta pointed out.

"She's my aunt," I said.

"And Roo is certainly not her name."

I hadn't thought about that. "It's not?"

"It's Myrtle Rudine," Retta said.

I made a face.

"Yep. Ridiculous names is how mothers curse their firstborn in these parts," Retta explained. "Thus I am Loretta Lipscomb."

"I'm sorry," I said. My eyeballs were starting to sting. "Is this enough?"

"Perfect," she told me. Was I dreaming? Nothing had ever been "perfect" to Loretta. She scraped the onions off the board into the sizzling butter. I heard Mama's bedroom door, then the bathroom door open and close. She'd be taking her famous half-hour shower.

"So what does Mamby have to do with Miss Scarlett?" I asked.

Loretta turned the onions, then dumped in the potatoes she'd diced.

"It sounds like *Mammy*," Loretta said. "And Scarlett has a faithful house slave by that name. Every plantation was supposed to have a mammy." Wrapping a dish towel around her head, Loretta crossed her arms out in front of her like she was resting them on big breasts, then said, "'I diapered three generations of Robillard girls and it sho' is a happy day!'"

I winced. "So Nissa is saying that calling her mother 'Mamby' is a throwback to slavery times?"

"Ah ha!" Retta said. "The sun is finally up."

"Is she right?"

"Set the table," she commanded.

"When you answer," I said again.

"It's more of a hand-me-down," she said. "More of a remnant."

"If I find the right name, do you think Nissa and I could be friends?" I asked, opening the cabinet, counting down the curves of three plates.

"What on earth for?" Nissa asked.

"I just thought, after I took her her supper, that she was the kind of person I'd like to get to know." I could feel the roots of my hair start to heat up. In a minute my whole face would be red. No. Scarlet.

"*Girl,*" Loretta said, flipping the hash browns. "She's a girl."

"I know that." I was hunting in the silverware drawer for forks that wouldn't leave that sharp taste in your mouth. I was hoping Loretta wouldn't see me blush.

"I'll bet you do," she said.

"What's that supposed to mean?"

She slid the potatoes onto a plate she had warmed in the oven, then set it back in. "Now the eggs," she said, lopping off another chunk of butter for the skillet. "It means," she said, tilting the pan and swirling the butter flow, "that slave owners' sons still get interested in Mammies' daughters."

Loretta might as well have punched me in the stomach. The breath went right out of me.

"Don't be a baby," she said, pouring in the eggs.

The sight of that yellow blob made me want to puke. "You make me sick!" I said, and started out of the kitchen.

"Whoa, White Boy!" Loretta called. "You make yourself sick."

"I do not," I said, turning in the doorway.

"Get me a bowl," Retta ordered. The eggs were fluffy now. They looked good. I got out the carnival glass bowl Deaton loved. "You just can't believe you're attracted to a colored girl."

"It's not *that*," I said, holding the golden vessel while Loretta spooned in the eggs. And then I said what I didn't know I knew. "I can't believe I'm attracted to *anybody*. It's never happened before." The truth was, I'd *thought* so much about Nissa that I'd hardly given myself a chance to *feel*. "The fact that she's colored just makes it more complicated. Even if she was Sudie Renfro"—a girl we knew from One-Way—"I wouldn't know what to do."

"Don't do ANYTHING," Loretta said. "Zero, zilch, nada. Can you manage that, Leon Bradshaw, or is it too simple for the likes of you?"

Just then Mama came into the kitchen, looking small in her fluffy pink robe.

"Smells great," she said. "Why don't you two stay up all night every night?"

"Only when Sonny blows his circuits," Loretta said.

"How do you feel, Sonny?" Mama asked.

I was so unsettled by my talk with Loretta that I answered without thinking. "Like a bucket of bolts."

twenty-five

We ate. Even Deaton had some, and he usually won't touch breakfast food that doesn't have milk or syrup on it. Mama went to work. I called Uncle Marty to ask if I could come in later in the day since I had to get some sleep. "You rest, Son," he said. "I'll have the pans soaking."

Loretta wouldn't consider a nap. "Only the dead sleep in the daylight," she said.

It seemed like as soon as I lay down and shut my eyes, I saw Daddy. He was standing at the bottom of a rock cliff, the face of it making stone stripes behind him, wearing the clothes he had worn on the day he left—gray pants, white shirt, khaki-colored suspenders. He waved to me and rocks began to roll down the cliff—at first just two or three and then a regular hailstorm of rocks, some big as baseballs. This didn't faze Daddy. He held his hand out in front of him and caught one that came over his head, then bit into it like an apple. Another one he bored a hole in with a finger, then pulled out a dark blue scarf to blow his nose on. Meanwhile, rocks were piling up around him and dark birds were swooping above him and I was trying to yell, "Get out of there! It's dangerous!" but I didn't have a voice. I tried to run toward him, only to find my feet stuck in a lake of chewing gum. I started to cry and my tears flew forward, sizzling as they hit the rocks. When one hit Daddy, he turned into a lizard about the size of a piano bench and skittered off. That's all I remembered.

I woke up at noon in a hot, still house. It wasn't Mamby's—Verna's—Whoever's—day to be here, so Deaton was at Aunt Joy's. The smell of onions and coffee hung in the air, and it was so quiet I could almost hear myself sweat.

Nothing to do but get up and take a shower, eat a sandwich, go to work.

I could walk to the Circle of Life in ten minutes or bike over in a flash. This day I walked. True to his word, Uncle Marty had saved me all the mixing bowls and donut trays, dough hooks and icing pitchers. Some were soaking in tepid gray water, but a lot more were stacked on counters and under the worktable.

"Thank the Lord you're here," Uncle Marty said when I went in the screen door at the back. "Dirty dishes are starting to swarm like locusts."

"Don't worry. Pharaoh and I will beat them down with a dishrag," I said.

Uncle Marty gave me a doubtful look. He can take his biblical references only so far. "Are you feeling better?" he asked.

"Yes sir. Just a little glazed."

He raised his flour-flecked eyebrows. "Glazed?"

I wanted to laugh but it didn't seem advisable.

"I mean *dazed*, I guess. Not much sleep."

"Well, it's good you don't have to work any machinery."

I nodded.

"So dig in."

I let out the cold water, rinsed down the industrial-size sink as best I could, and refilled it with hot water. Wash, scrub, wash, rinse, dry. Over and over and over. There were lunch dishes, too, because while the sandwiches are served in paper-lined plastic baskets, canned soup and coffee rate thick bowls and mugs.

As I worked I thought about the menu board, how much more fun it had been to paint that than to wash dishes. Even doing the scripture, which was tedious. Twice I'd messed up "O set me on a rock," once by making a blob when I had too much black on my brush and once when I put *ne* instead of *me.* I tried to add the rest of the *m*, but it filled up the space between words. So I had to let it dry, paint it white, let it dry, start again. I was tense till I got the whole sentence out: "O set me on the rock that is higher than I."

Remembering that made me almost remember something else. *Rock*, rock that is higher—yes! My dream. Daddy standing there while the cliff threw itself at him, rock by rock. What was that about?

The lunch rush was over by the time I got everything put away and the sink scrubbed. Uncle Marty came in to check on me.

"How well did you know my daddy?" I asked him. The shock of saying that sent a chill over me. Hey! I thought. This is one way to cool off.

Uncle Marty cleared his throat. "Well enough," he said.

"For how long?"

"From when we were boys. My youngest brother, Wickliffe, is Leon's age, and they were friends, so sometimes we all did things together."

"Like what?"

Uncle Marty looked around like he'd never been in the Circle of Life before and was checking for a fire exit. He took a deep breath. "The pastimes of all boys," he said. "Baseball, frog-gigging, catching minnows and salamanders down in White Pine Creek. Don't you and Deaton play there?"

"Salamanders?" My voice went high, then low. "I mean yes, we do, but aren't salamanders sort of like lizards?"

"Their shapes are a little different. Haven't you ever waded the creek to catch them?"

"Sure," I said. "But mine always get away."

twenty-six

Later, walking home, I felt like I was moving through spider-webs. I couldn't get out of these sticky questions: Where was Daddy? Why did he write to Uncle Marty? Why couldn't I ask? And for that matter, why couldn't I be friends with Nissa? What kind of world is this anyway?

When I turned down Rhubarb, I could see Deaton sitting on the front steps. Poor kid! I thought. He knows even less than I do. That's pathetic.

He seemed to be looking at something on our front walk, so I didn't holler at him when I got closer. In fact, I tried to be as quiet as I could so I could sneak up on him. It worked. When I was just a couple of feet away, I said, "Deaton!" real loud, and he jumped like he was hiccuping all over. I laughed.

"That's not funny, Sonny."

Then I really laughed.

"You should see yourself when you have a spell."

That stopped me. "What are you looking at?" I asked him.

"Ants swarming," he said.

And for some reason, though I could see the almost-orange ants pouring slowly across the sidewalk, what I pictured was Aunt Roo and Aunt Joy, one carrying a leaf-bit big as a sail and the other a car-size piece of bread, bumping into each other as they struggled across the road. I started laughing again.

"What's wrong with you?" Deaton asked.

"I'm punch-drunk," I said. "From staying up all night. So when you said 'ants,' I pictured *our* aunts—you know, Roo and Joy."

"With six legs?"

"Yep," I said, and Deaton started laughing too.

"Would they live in an 'aunthill'?" he asked.

"Oh yes," I told him. "With a screened-in porch and a grape arbor." These were Aunt Roo's and Aunt Joy's treasures.

"Sonny?" Deaton's voice turned serious again. "A man called today. He asked for you."

"Who was it?"

"I don't know. I told him you were at work."

"Well, who did it sound like?" I asked him. "Somebody from One-Way?"

"I don't think so because he said, 'Who is this?' and when I told him, he was so quiet I thought he was gone till he said, 'Lord God, Deaton!' and hung up."

My heart sort of slid sideways. "That was Daddy," I told him.

"*Our* daddy?" Deaton jumped up and got right in my face. "Where is he?"

"Calm down. I don't know. Somewhere they've got telephones."

"Why does he want to talk to you?"

"I don't know that, either," I said, but I did know. Raymond and Eddie must have told him I'd shown up at their door.

"He should have asked for Mama," Deaton declared. Poor squashed kid! It didn't occur to him that the father who hadn't seen him since his bassinet days should have talked to him.

"'Should' doesn't mean much when it comes to Daddy," I said.

twenty-seven

Next morning when I entered the kitchen, Nissa's mama was there. I didn't have a clue about what to call her. She was washing down the cabinets.

"Morning, Sonny," she said. "Biscuits in the oven."

"Thanks," I said. "Is Nissa out of the hospital?"

Mamby/Verna/Mrs. Preece turned around and for a second she looked the way she did at the hospital, like her heart was heavy as a cannonball.

"She's home but she ain't really with us yet."

"Why not?" I asked.

"We got legs," Nissa's mama said.

"Could I come see her?" Was my tongue not connected to my brain anymore?

Just then Deaton came shuffling into the kitchen in

his pj's. He went right up to Mamby—I *hate* not knowing what to call her—put his arms around her waist, and leaned his head into her stomach. She patted his hair. "Morning, sleepyhead," she said.

I wanted to be back where Deaton was, not thinking, not chopped up in questions. It's like you sleepwalk your whole childhood and the world seems fine the way it is— no, it doesn't "seem" anything. It just *is*, easy as pie. And then you get old as me and you wake up.

"Deaton, honey," she said, "let go and let Mamby check on the biscuits." He unwrapped himself from her and slid into a chair. She opened the oven just enough to see, then reached for a pot holder. I got up and took the breadbasket off the top of the refrigerator and handed it to her.

"Thank you, Sonny. You're handy as a pocket in a shirt."

I opened a drawer to find a napkin for the basket. "Forgot that," I said.

She looked at me like she saw something she hadn't seen before. Deaton and I took our places at the table. A few minutes later I was marveling at how Deaton managed to get honey on his forehead as well as his biscuit and plate and the table when Nissa's mama said, "So how come you want to visit my girl?"

Don't ask me that! I wanted to say. I just have to see her again. I just keep thinking about her. . . .

"I've been thinking about her since I took her her dinner," I said, edging out word by word like I was walking on a rotten roof. "If it was me that had . . . that it had happened to, I'd need some company."

"Nissa's friends are good to stop by," her mama said, and gave me that look again.

"I guess I want to be her friend," I said. Oh Lord, I'd done it now. Just don't let wild-mouth Loretta show up. . . .

"You do, do you?" she asked.

I nodded.

"Whooee!" she said, and did something I had never seen her do in our house before. She took a biscuit out of the basket, curled a little butter off the top of the pat with a knife, inserted that in the biscuit without cutting it in two, and took a bite. All the food she had cooked in that house and I'd never before seen her eat. That seemed so wrong I said something else I'd had no intention of saying.

"I don't know what to call you anymore."

"He's going to have a spell," Deaton said, golden crumbs wreathing his mouth.

"I *am* not," I said. "It's just that, well, 'Mamby' seems disrespectful—Nissa thinks it is—and I can't call you by your first name, can I? And Mrs. . . . ." I hesitated, still not sure whether it was Preece or Peak.

"Preece," she said, standing completely still, hands clasped in front of her, the blue dish towel folded over her left arm between wrist and elbow. "Sonny, honey," she started, and all of a sudden I had to blink back tears. "I been feeding and hugging you since the day you was born. Far as I'm concerned, you're a little light, but you're mine. You can't call me *Mama*—you got Selma. So *Mamby* suits me just fine. It's a baby name came out of Loretta's mouth."

"Oh," I said, and my tears were winked away in the satisfaction that Loretta had started the name in the first place.

"And I guess if you want to see Nissa—and if she *will* see you, *and* if Selma says you can, which I don't for one breath believe she will—that's possible. But I want you to think on something first."

"What's that?" I asked, and then noticed Deaton looking at Mamby, amazed. She didn't sound like herself.

"It's not far from this house to mine, from Rhubarb to Staniford Road, but the ground is about as slippery as ground can get."

"Not now," Deaton said. "It's dusty."

"Sonny knows what I mean," Mamby said.

I did and I didn't. Or at least I didn't want to. "Thanks, Mamby," I said.

She rested her hand first on my head, then on my shoulder. "Nissa's got notions," she said. "Gets them from Freelan." She turned back to the sink and ran the water to fill the dishpan. "Freelan's been to Montgomery and Mobile. Tasted tomorrow, so he turns up his nose at today."

"He still wants to marry Nissa, though?"

"Swears he does," Mamby said. "But Nissa don't believe it. And anyhow, she says there's no call for a one-legged girl to marry."

"Won't she get a fake leg?" Deaton asked.

"Yes sir," Mamby said. "But that won't do her no good if she won't stand up, if she won't go on walking."

"I'll come see her," I said.

"Maybe, maybe not," Mamby replied.

twenty-eight

When the call came, I was lying on the glider watching a mud dauber start a nest next to the porch light. I'd come home from the Circle of Life, felt smothered in the steamy house, and gotten a glass of tea to take outside.

I'd had maybe two sips when Deaton pushed open the screen door. "The phone again," he said.

I sat up. "Is it—?"

"I think so."

I scrambled to my feet and through the living room, which seemed dark after the billion-watt sun. The phone was in a little alcove in the hall wall.

"Hello," I said.

No answer.

"This is Sonny." Silence. "Hello?"

"Sonny," the voice said, smooth and low. "I hear you've been looking for me."

I started to shake. After all these years, that voice still held sweat and aftershave. "I did come to Mobile," I said.

"So Raymond told me."

"Daddy—uh, Dad . . ." Man! I didn't know what to call *him*, either. "I just wanted to talk to you." That was lame.

"Talk away."

"But it's not . . . ," I began. "It's . . . well, I don't know. I guess I need to see you."

"Ah!" he said. What kind of answer is "Ah"?

"I'm thirteen," I told him.

"I know."

He was so calm I wanted to scream, but instead I said, "Loretta's getting wild."

"Loretta was *born* wild," he said.

"Don't you care?" I hated the whine in my voice, but at least I'd got out the real question.

He laughed. And the rush of anger that came over me made the narrow hallway close in. No! I told myself, like a mental slap in the face. You won't do that.

"I do care," the man who had been my daddy said. "But caring about Loretta doesn't mean you can *do* anything about her. That was clear by the time she was six months old."

"You could *be* here," I said, grateful for the phone.

Not having to actually face him gave me courage.

"No, I couldn't, Sonny."

"Why not?" I practically hollered into the receiver. Mamby leaned in from the kitchen, eyebrows raised. I waved her away.

"When you're older—"

"When I'm older, it'll be too late to have a daddy. I won't want to talk to you then!"

"Son . . ." Was that pain in his voice?

"And you wouldn't recognize me anyway!" I slammed down the phone, then marched through the kitchen, where Mamby was mixing up salmon croquettes for Mama to fry later. Cantaloupe was standing on her hind legs in hopes of getting a bite.

"Easy," Mamby said.

Usually I like salmon, but right then it smelled awful. I went out the back door and just kept walking. Past the end of our yard, into the brambles that somebody said was a power-line easement, only we didn't have that power yet. Then instead of walking straight through to where the brush thins out and the land slopes to the creek, I turned left and headed away from town, deeper into the thicket.

Part of the brambles are blackberry canes, and I got lashed by their thorny whips. Another part is bindweed that lassos your ankle and can jerk you down if you're not careful—and "careful" was the last word for me right then. I wanted to howl when I hit the ground. I even tried—who would hear me?—but what came out sounded like a rusty gate opening.

Part of me was cursing myself for hanging up without finding out where Daddy was, and another part was cursing myself for caring. And then there was the part that felt responsible for him leaving in the first place. If I hadn't watched Mama throw that tray at him, if I hadn't heard them fight . . . "You see why I have to leave," he'd said. "A man can't live in a house of spies." I kept walking.

The second time the bindweed caught my shoe, I realized it before I pitched forward. And while I stopped to get free, it was quiet enough to hear voices.

"Put me down!" a girl was saying. "Put me down right now!"

"Now baby—" That was a man.

"I hate you, Freelan Diggs!"

Oh my God! I crept forward and peered through the green loops and snarls. He had set her on a mossy spot by the creek and was squatting down in front of her.

"You got to marry me, Nissa. I love you just like always."

"And how could I marry some fool would come steal me out of my house?"

"I had to do that, sugar. I couldn't stay closed in that room and you not breathing a word."

"So that gives you the right to kidnap me—?"

"I figured being by the creek would do you good," Freelan explained. "The world's still out here, baby, just as sweet as the day we went fishing."

"Except now I'm missing a leg."

"And oh, honey, I'm missing you!"

In one smooth movement, Freelan was on his knees, had his arms around Nissa, and was kissing her. His back was so broad that I couldn't see her anymore. It wasn't fair! He had his arms around her like I wanted to—my whole body knew that now. His mouth on her soft mouth. Then he pulled back. Had she slapped him? No, she was crying. Making big, ugly sounds.

I shouldn't *be* here, I thought. I shouldn't *see* this. But I wanted to. This might be as close to Nissa as I'd ever get. And besides, if I tried to leave, they'd hear me and Freelan might—oh, Lord . . .

"Nissa, Nissa," Freelan Diggs said, like he was soothing a baby. He had her in his arms again and was rocking a little.

"Sing to me," she said, her breath rough with tears. "But no love stuff."

There was a pause and then his voice, rich and deep:

Rock my soul
In the bosom of Abraham
Rock my soul
In the bosom of Abraham

Rock my soul
In the bosom of Abraham
O rock my soul!

So high, can't get over it
So low, can't get under it
So wide, can't get 'round it
O rock my soul!

As he started the chorus again, Nissa joined in, singing a different part:

Rock my soul
In the bosom of Abraham . . .

When their voices touched, something happened. Time got real slow or real fast or opened up and it was like they had already been married and had kids and lived and died, like everything was over and happening and about to happen, all the perfect things and the hateful things, too, the singing and the creek and the poison fishhooks.

It was too much. I had to get out of there, noise or no noise. I crouched down and crept the first little ways and then ran, as much as a person can run through brambles. I doubt they noticed. They were too far gone with love and singing.

twenty-nine

When I got home Loretta had taken my place on the glider. I had thought to go in the front to avoid Mama or Mamby, whichever one was in the kitchen.

Hearing me on the steps, Loretta looked over. "Who threw *you* in the brier patch?"

"This is nothing," I said.

Loretta swung her legs over the side of the yellow cushion and sat up. She had on a bright green-and-white checked dress, like something a rabbit might dream. "Compared to what?"

"The emptiness of life," I said. I didn't really feel that life was empty, though, just that other people had the full part.

"Sonny the Philosopher!" Loretta declared. "You over your spell?"

The way she put that gave it a whole new dimension.

Was I under a spell? Who cast it? Was I doomed to keep acting in certain hopeless ways? Or could I break it? Maybe searching for Daddy was me trying to break it. Or dreaming about Nissa. Then I had an awful thought: What if my spell was me?

"Evidently not," Loretta said.

"Not what?"

"Evidently you're not over your spell."

"No," I said, and watched the brightness go out of Loretta's face. Why she was looking for a fight! Well, she wouldn't get it from me. "I may never get over it," I said.

At this Loretta leapt up and began bowing an invisible violin.

"Oh, give it a rest," I told her.

She flopped back down. "So where have you been?"

"Down to the creek," I said, sitting in the Tulip Chair.

"Through a bale of bob-wire?"

"Yeah."

"Sonny," Loretta said, turning to face me. She had drawn around her eyes with something black like Cleopatra in our social studies book. "What kind of trouble are you looking for?"

And just like that, I said, "I was looking for Daddy."

"In the creek?"

I didn't care if she was mocking me. I felt like a car with two flats. "No," I said. "In Mobile."

"All right!" Loretta exclaimed, clapping her hands

once, then knotting her fingers together. "Sonny the Sleuth! Did you find him?"

I shook my head.

"How did you know where to look?"

"I had an address."

"From?" She stretched the word out, coaxing me.

And I stuck. If I told Loretta about Uncle Marty's letter, Lord only knew what she would do. She always said the only thing holy about him was the donuts.

"Never mind," I said. "But I did find some men who knew him."

"What did they tell you?"

"Nothing. They—"

At that moment Deaton came out the screen door. Holding a big soda cracker that he appeared to be licking rather than eating, he walked over and pushed back Loretta's feet to make room for himself on the glider.

"What are you talking about?" Deaton asked.

"*You*," Loretta answered.

But I said, "Daddy."

Loretta scowled at me, her rusty eyebrows scrunched up.

"What did he say?" Deaton asked.

"Who?" Loretta wanted to know.

"Daddy," I said. "He called here. That's why I went to the creek."

"What did he want?" Loretta asked.

"He wants me to quit looking for him," I said. "At least till I'm older."

"He's not worth the shoe leather," Loretta said.

"But he's our *daddy,*" Deaton insisted.

"Hell of a lot of good that's done us," I put in.

"Oooooh, Sonny talks Man Talk!" Loretta said in her female impersonator voice. Then she backed down. "You're right, though."

"So are you going to?" Deaton asked.

"Going to what?"

"Stop looking for him."

"I don't know," I told them.

"I do," Loretta said. "You won't be happy till you find him, and then you'll be miserable."

"Thanks," I said, just as Mama came out on the porch.

"Good Lord," she said. "My entire brood."

We blinked. Nothing to say.

She sighed. "Wash up for dinner." Nobody moved. "Come on now. I don't want it to get cold."

"Cold?" Loretta said.

Even Mama laughed. In the swelter of Mozier July, "cold" sounded great.

thirty

While we were eating our supper of croquettes, collard greens, and orange Jell-O with pineapple, Nell Kivitt and her family were moving in down the street. Moving into Mr. Boatman's house, which had been empty since he died over a year ago. Mama said his children were fighting over who got what, so the paint had peeled off, the yard had grown up, and the ivy was licking the windows.

"I hope they're not renters," Mama said when Loretta told us she had seen the moving van drive in.

"Why?" I asked.

"You take better care of something if you own it," Mama said.

"The license plate on their station wagon says Massachusetts," Loretta put in.

"Lord help us!" Mama exclaimed. "Yankees."

Loretta rolled her eyes.

"Do they have a boy?" Deaton wanted to know.

"Don't know. I haven't seen hide nor hair of them," Mama told him.

"I think they do," Deaton said. "If they have a station wagon."

"They probably have a dog, too," I said, "big as a coffee table."

"And the mother's name is Peregrine," Loretta ventured. "And the dad is Bronson, like Loser May Alcott's."

"Maybe the son's name *is* Loser," I suggested.

"He's a twin," Loretta said. "His brother is Upchuck."

Deaton started giggling.

"They moved here from East Runaway," Loretta went on.

Mama put her knife and fork down. "This has gone far enough," she said. "You're ridiculing that poor family and it's not right, even if they *are* Yankees."

"How do you know they're poor?" Retta challenged.

"I mean it hurts to have people who've never even seen you laughing at you."

"But they don't know," Deaton insisted.

"Names stick," Mama said. "You call a boy 'Loser' sight unseen and that's what you'll think when you meet him. It hurts ahead of time."

Mama's cheeks were red, and she sat up straighter in

defense of her principles. "So by way of apology," she continued, "I want us to take them the peach cobbler Joy sent over."

"What?!" Loretta shrieked. "I was going to give Wesley some of that when he comes to pick me up."

"Give him some Jell-O," Mama said, returning glare for glare.

"Well, don't expect *me* to take it to them," Retta said. "I've got to get ready for a date." She put her hands on the table and stood up so fast her chair fell over. It hit the floor like a gunshot.

"Not till you clean up the kitchen, you don't," Mama said. "Sonny and Deaton can carry it down there."

This was Loretta's signal to get red in the face and yell and flail her freckled arms, but for some cause she didn't. Maybe the heat had taken it out of her.

Deaton noticed this too. As we walked down the street with the Pyrex dish of peach cobbler wrapped in wax paper and the lightning bugs just starting to wink, he asked, "How come Loretta didn't fight?"

"Maybe her stomach hurt," I said. "She didn't eat a lot either." Maybe the news about Daddy upset her, I thought. Could that be possible? Could Loretta *care*?

When we got to the Boatman place Deaton said, "I better go home. I forgot to feed Cantaloupe."

"Oh, no," I said. "You're not running out on me."

"But my cat—"

"She won't starve."

"We don't even *know* these people," Deaton whined.

"That's the point," I said as we started up the steps.

"And the house might be haunted."

"I don't think so," I said, knocking on the frame of the screen door. The front door was open. I peered in but all I could see in the darkness was boxes.

A little girl came to the door, her brown hair in pigtails. She had on white shorts and a red T-shirt with a heart stitched in white. She stared at us with her finger in her mouth, then called out, "Nell!" and ran back into the gloom.

In a few minutes an older girl appeared. Her hair was blond, cut like a cap, and she had very blue eyes. Hot as it was, she was wearing blue jeans and a long-sleeved white T-shirt that said BOSTON GARDENS on it. She looked older than Loretta, but her breasts were too small to stretch the letters. "Hello," she said. "I'm Nell Kivitt."

"I'm Sonny," I said, "and this is my brother Deaton. We're the Bradshaws from down the street—the little yellow house. And Mama sent you this cobbler."

Nell looked uncertain.

"Pie," I explained.

"She didn't make it," Deaton said. "Aunt Joy did."

"How kind," Nell said, like she was somebody's

grandmother. She opened the screen door just enough to take our offering. As she did, I noticed her wrists, thin as wands. "Willowy" came into my head. She was willowy.

"Do you have any boys?" Deaton asked.

"Please?" she said.

"He wants to know if you have a brother he could play with," I told her.

Nell laughed, but not very much. "I *do* have a brother," she said. "But I'm afraid he won't do you much good. We're twins."

"Loretta *said* that," Deaton started, but just then a man called from deep in the house.

"Who is it, Nell?"

"Neighbors, Father," she answered over her shoulder, then turned to me. "Thank you, Danny—"

"Sonny," I said.

"And *Deaton*," he put in.

"Thank you both," she said, clearly done with us.

"Mama says welcome to Mozier," I told her.

"It's friendly," Nell said, like you might say something was poison. And she turned and disappeared.

As we walked home, Deaton declared, "She's a vampire. And she couldn't ask us in because those boxes are coffins and her brother is in one of them and—"

"Deaton, where did you get that idea?" The last I'd

heard his big fear was of pirates who came up the creek and captured little boys to work on their ships.

"Albion told me," Deaton said.

"Told you what?"

"That that house was a vampire place. They drank Mr. Boatman's blood."

"Don't pay any attention to Albion. You know he makes things up to scare you."

"There aren't any vampires?"

"No, Deaton."

"You're sure."

"Mmm-hmm."

"How about zombies?"

"Nope." We turned up the walk at our house.

"How about queers?"

"What?!" The change in my voice scared him, but I couldn't help it.

"Albion said the queers got Daddy."

"Oh, my God!" I said, stopping in front of my brother, putting my hands on his shoulders. "Deaton, Albion is just *mean*, do you understand? He makes stuff up so he can hurt people. Don't listen to him. And if he tells you stuff anyway, come check it out with me. Don't go worrying about it."

"Okay," Deaton said.

But all the time I was telling him this I was thinking

about another door I'd gone to and stood at and not been invited in, about Raymond and Eddie. Were they—

"Sonny," Deaton said, interrupting my thoughts. "What's a queer?"

I felt like my insides had turned into mop water. It was all I could do to get over to the glider and sit. Deaton plopped down beside me.

"Well?" he said.

I shook my head.

"Don't you know?"

"It's not that," I said, although it sort of *was* that. I mean, nobody had ever *told* me what the word meant. When Uncle Sink had given me the birds-and-bees talk (or the pipes-and-fittings, as he called it) he'd said, "Never let a queer near you." I'd asked how I'd recognize one and he just said, "Believe me, a man puts the moves on you, you'll know." How could I tell Deaton that? Especially since it was our daddy he was asking about.

"If you don't tell me, I'll go ask Mama," he threatened.

"That would be the world's *worst* idea," I said.

"So you tell me." Deaton was kicking the front of the glider with the heels of his Keds and making it jerk back and forth, the exact wrong motion for my mop-water insides.

"Stop it!" I said.

He did.

I took a deep breath. I looked up at the porch light to see how the mud dauber was doing on its nest. Progress. "Okay," I said. "But Deaton, before I tell you what it means you've got to swear to two things."

"I swear," Deaton said solemnly.

"Not yet!" I protested. "You don't even know what they are."

"So tell me."

"The first one is, do not tell anybody what I tell you. Not cousins, not aunts or uncles—that includes Marty—not Grandma or Mamby or Mama. *Especially* not Mama. You understand?"

"Yes sir," he said. "But can I tell Cantaloupe?"

Lord, I thought, this is how ridiculous a situation I'm in—explaining "queer" to a kid so young he wants to tell his cat.

"You can," I said. "But not out loud. And second, you must promise NOT to think what this word means is true about Daddy. Albion is just—"

"You already said that." Deaton was giving me a look I'd seen Loretta give Mama. How come she had these two fiery kids and, in between, the mop water?

"Okay. Swear."

"I swear."

"On the Bible."

"I swear on the Bible."

"And the Holy Name of Jesus," I said.

"Oh, come on, Sonny."

"Do it."

"I swear on the Holy Name of Jesus," he said, then sighed and shrugged.

"No fingers crossed?"

Deaton shook his head.

"Toes?"

"No!"

"All right, calm down," I said. "This is important."

"You don't want to tell me," Deaton said, his eyes stormy.

"No, I don't, but I guess I've got to, so here it is." I took another deep breath. I looked at the morning glories all closed tight on the trellis at the side of the porch. Then I said, "A man is called a 'queer' when he loves men."

"Loves them?" Deaton asked, his face sort of squinched.

"Loves them the way most men love women. You know, mates with them." Ugh. There. I'd said it.

"Mates with them?" I could tell from the tone of Deaton's voice that he didn't have a clue. Well, he was only seven.

"Deaton, do you know where babies come from?"

"Mama got me at the hospital," he said. "But Mamby

said somebody brings hers to the house. Her granny, I think."

I rolled my eyes up at what would have been the heavens if it wasn't the porch ceiling and the mud daubers.

"Not exactly," I told him.

"How then?"

"Look," I said. "I'm going in to tell Mama we're back and I'll get us some tea."

"You're running off!"

"Not a chance," I said.

When I got back with the aluminum tumblers of tea, Deaton hadn't moved. I handed him his.

"You know the difference between boys and girls?" I asked.

He took a sip of tea. "Girls don't have wieners," he said.

"Right," I said. Oh Lord, this was so pathetic. What was I supposed to say now? It was getting dark. June bugs who didn't know it was July were dive-bombing the light, and I was about to say, and did say, "They don't have a wiener but they have something that it fits in."

"A bun?" Deaton asked.

That did it! I started laughing and I kept laughing and the tea was sloshing so much I had to set it on the porch. The more I tried to stop—because Deaton did not look amused *at all*—the worse it got, till I bent over and put my head on my knees, and Deaton, furious, started pounding me on the back, but I went on with these whoops of laughter because, God, a wiener and a bun! And who should arrive at this out-of-control scene but Loretta and Wesley the Great.

"Is he having a fit?" Loretta asked Deaton.

"No," he said, giving me the hardest wallop yet. "He's supposed to tell me—"

I sat up. "I will, Deaton. I will."

"Will tell him what?" Retta demanded.

"We're trying to have a man-to-man talk here, Loretta, if you'll just excuse us."

"Well, *we're* trying to have a little man-to-woman talk," she countered. "You should go to your room."

"Are you going to mate?" Deaton asked.

"Good God!" Wesley exclaimed.

Loretta leaned down and pinched me on the forearm, hard. "Scram!" she said.

Once we got to our room, I closed the door and said, "Just give me a chance here, Deaton. This isn't easy."

"Get to Daddy," he insisted.

"It's *not* about Daddy," I said.

"Okay. Queers."

Deaton climbed up to sit on his bed, so I did too. Malcolm, the teddy bear that had been Loretta's, then mine, lay on the pillow along with the orange snake I won at the carnival. Cantaloupe was curled up next to it.

"Girls have a place inside where the boy's wiener fits, and when grown-ups do that, it's called "mating," and that starts babies."

"Why?"

"Because there are seeds that come out of the man into the woman," I said.

"Girls are gardens?"

"Sort of."

"I'd never get that close to one," he said.

"Maybe not now," I told him. "But someday."

"Men don't have that bun place," Deaton said.

"That's right. They do something else. I'm not sure what."

"So do they come and get people?"

"Who?"

"Queers."

"No, of course not! They—they find each other, I guess, like men and women do."

"So who found Daddy?"

"Deaton!" I could feel the anger hot on the back of my neck. "Didn't you hear me? Daddy is *not* a queer. *Nobody* got him. He left for his own reasons. None of us knows why. But I do know one thing: I'm going to beat the shit out of Albion."

Deaton looked skeptical. "Can I watch?"

thirty-one

The next day at the Circle of Life I worked fast and furious, trying not to think. Scrubbing was good, a way to get rid of what you don't want. Sweeping was useful too—reach into dark corners with the broom, pull out what's fallen down there to rot. No need to examine it. Just out of the darkness and into the garbage. Make it clean, even the baseboards.

"Who lit a fire under you?" Uncle Marty asked.

"Nobody," I said, thinking Deaton, thinking Albion. "I just figure this needs a good going-over." Mama's words. I was surprised to hear them come out of my mouth.

"Well, if you run out of dirt to attack here, you can always go over to my kitchen."

"Yes sir," I said. The truth was, we'd never been to

Marty's, though he'd had dinner at our house several times a week since the summer Daddy left. I knew he had an apartment at the Callahans' over on Gardenia, but I had never darkened the door. Was that strange or was there some kind of woman-man rule, like the colored-white rule, which said he could come to our house but we couldn't go to his? Were there lots more hidden rules I didn't know yet?

Hidden, I thought. *Hid in.* Uncle Marty hid Daddy's letter in his calendar in the drawer beneath the counter. I could go anytime and get it. More to the point, he hid the fact that Daddy wrote to him, that they were in touch when Mama and Daddy weren't. *In touch*—what a crazy way to say people write letters, as if they laid word-hands on each other.

I was filling the mop bucket as I thought this and I didn't want to think any further. I tried hard to turn my mind around and go somewhere else with it. I read the back of the floor-cleaner bottle. I found the place where the bucket was stamped with how many gallons it would hold. The numbers were pressed into the metal—tin?—so they were raised. You could feel them like Braille. Braille Bucket, I thought. Blind mopping. But that brought me back to what I couldn't see though it was right in front of me. I couldn't get away from it.

If Uncle Marty was who he seemed to be—a faithful friend of a poor abandoned family—wouldn't he tell us any news he had from Daddy? Wouldn't he have shared it with us all these years?

Wait a minute, I told myself. You don't KNOW he didn't tell your mother. It could be just you kids who are left in the dark. But I didn't think so. Why would Mama keep something like that quiet? She used to boast about the checks coming. She used to act like any scrap of paper Daddy wrote on was sacred.

But that was a long time ago, when she had hope that he might write to us, when she still insisted he'd be coming home. If she knew he wrote to Uncle Marty she'd be furious; she'd have to know why. Or was *I* the one that had to know? Maybe Mama would just cling to Uncle Marty as a source of information. Maybe that was their bond.

I looked at Uncle Marty's back. He was making hamburger patties. Twenty-five a day, that's what we did. If we didn't sell them all, the extras went in the freezer. If we needed more, they came out of there. But the first twenty-five were always fresh. Uncle Marty was getting so fat he was starting to look stuffed. It wasn't just that his clothes were too small but that his SKIN was too tight. His neck had a double roll. And he was whistling "Higher Ground." We sing it every Sunday at One-Way, so I could fill in the words:

Lord, lift me up and let me stand
by faith on Heaven's tableland,

a higher plane than I have found.

Lord, plant my feet on higher ground.

Still trying to distract myself, I thought, Lifting *you* would be a challenge, but then I pictured a strong man like Daddy with his arms around Uncle Marty, and all of a sudden black spots swam in front of my eyes and I felt like I was going over backward. I didn't, though. I grabbed the edge of the sink and broke into Uncle Marty's song. "What the hell is going on here?" I demanded.

He turned around very slowly. "Sonny! What has come over you?" he asked.

"I know you write to my daddy," I said. "I know you know where he is."

Uncle Marty's whole face blinked and then he drew back and his expression flashed from fear to anger. "Have you been TRESPASSING, Sonny Bradshaw?"

I ignored that.

"Do I have to tell your mama and your One-Way family that you are a boy who cannot be trusted?"

I took a step toward him. "What's Mama going to say when she finds out Daddy writes to you? What would One-Way folks say? I bet you know why he left. I bet you've known all along—you may even have had something to do with it."

Before I could figure out why I'd said that, Marty lunged forward and grabbed me by the shoulders. He pressed his thumbs into my neck just above my collar-bones.

"You ungrateful and conniving boy!" He spat the words out. "If you attempt to defile my name, you'll have the whole church condemning you."

He's scared, I told myself. He sounds meaner than he is. But he was hurting my neck something fierce. "Let go of me!" I ordered. He did. And there we stood: face-to-face, sweat-drenched, shaking with anger, in matching white aprons. I looked Martin Bonner right in the eye and said: "Tell me where Daddy is and why he left and I won't tell a soul how I found out."

Uncle Marty drew himself up. "You presume to *bribe* me, Sonny Boy? You think I have no more backbone than that?"

"I think you have *secrets*," I said, the word surprising me as much as it did him. "I think you'd give a lot to keep it that way." I sounded cool as Loretta, but my heart was flopping like a fish. I held my breath. Uncle Marty seemed to hold his, too. We just stood there.

Finally he said, in a voice I hadn't heard before, "Go home. Keep your mouth shut. Tell Selma I need you to help with some things after I close. Then come back and we'll talk."

I let out my breath, then breathed in slowly. "Okay," I said.

"Okay?" he said, his voice rising. "What happened to 'Yes sir'?"

"I don't know what happened, sir. To you or to my daddy. That's what I'm trying to find out."

"Go!" he commanded, lifting his arm and pointing out the back, for all the world like the angel throwing Adam and Eve out of the Garden. But it was the Circle of Life I was leaving, Uncle Marty's sweet and greasy excuse for spreading the Word.

I wanted to go straight to the Chat 'n' Chew and tell Loretta all that had happened. I needed strengthening. But I'd agreed to keep my mouth shut for the time being. You're on your own, Sonny, I said to myself. And a voice inside replied, Like always.

thirty-two

I was home from the Circle of Life way early. Today I had ridden. I leaned my bike against the side of the garage, careful not to get it in Mama's flowers. There was no point in putting it away, since I'd be heading back soon. The kitchen window was open, and once the bike and I stopped rattling, I could hear Mamby's song:

> Do Lord, oh do Lord
> Oh, do remember me.
> Hallelujah!

Mamby's voice is big, like I think a cathedral would be, only warm.

Look away, beyond the blue.

I knew she was alone or she wouldn't be singing like that—she'd just hum under her breath. She was singing at her work just like the bees beside me were buzzing in the daylilies. At least *something* was right in this crazy mixed-up world; something was how it should be.

Yeah, a little voice in the back of my head said. Right for you, but how about for Mamby?

I can't stand this, I thought. I can't stand everything being different from how it looks, how it used to be. So I hurried in the back door and found Mamby in the bathroom, down on her knees, scrubbing the tub and singing.

I got a home in glory land
that outshines the sun.

"Mamby," I interrupted, coming up behind her. "Are you miserable?"

"Lord have mercy, child," she said, putting one hand on the tub rim and one on the toilet lid to help herself up. "You scared a year off this old life."

"I'm sorry," I said. "I just have to know."

"Let me finish this and we'll talk in the kitchen, Sonny. It's too small in here."

167

In a few minutes, Mamby poured me some lemonade and I sat down at the table.

"You're asking if *I'm* miserable?"

I nodded.

"Sometimes I'm a bit put out, but I'm not miserable. Not if Nissa will walk," she said. "If she'll welcome the life the Lord give her, I'll be fine, better than fine." She paused. "Now what's got you to thinking on misery?"

"I can't tell you," I said.

"Mmm-hmm," she said, setting the lemonade back in the Frigidaire. "That'll make you sick."

"Lemonade?"

"No, honey. Secrets."

And before I could think about it, I put my head down on my sweaty arms and cried.

Mamby rested her hand on my shoulder and said, "Good. If you can't get it out in words, get it out in water."

I cried on till I felt wrung out. When I sat back up, Mamby was standing on the other side of the table cutting corn off the cob.

"Better?" she asked.

"Yes," I said, my voice husky.

"Your mama won't let you see Nissa?"

"It's not that," I said, taking a paper napkin from the holder in the middle of the table. "I haven't even talked to her yet. It's other stuff." I turned my head away from the table and blew my nose.

"Nissa's a good one to talk to," Mamby said. She had all the kernels off the cob and was scraping it to get the milk out. It spattered some—on her brown arm, on the ivy-bordered plastic place mats, on the salt and pepper shakers. She looked at me looking at her. "Sometimes you got to make a mess to make something good. You know what I mean, Sonny?"

"Yes, Mamby," I said, and got that ache in my throat again. I felt halfway understood and I hadn't even told her anything. "Thank you."

"Anytime," she said.

I looked at the clock. Three-thirty. Uncle Marty would be getting ready to close—the Circle of Life didn't serve supper during the week. "Would you tell Mama I might be late for dinner?" I asked Mamby. "Uncle Marty wants me to help with some extra stuff after he closes."

"I'll tell Selma," Mamby said.

"I don't think I'll be too long," I offered.

"Good," Mamby said, and I realized I loved hearing her say that. I wanted to give her a hug.

"I'll just wash up," I said, ducking out to the bathroom.

In the kitchen with Mamby I had felt safe and solid, but once I left her I started shaking. I had no idea what I was doing, what a mess I'd got myself in. "To make something good"? Oh, Mamby, if only you're right!

I washed my face in cool water. My eyes were puffed

up but there was nothing I could do about it, and anyway, that was the least of my problems. I put my hand on the wall just at the point where the deep green tile met the light green paint. There's an end to everything, I thought. One way or another, I'll be home soon. One-Way! I started shaking again, then all at once I thought, What would Loretta say? Almost as if she were there, I heard, "Move it, Sonny. If you don't get on the road, you'll miss the car wreck." I just about smiled. With Mamby on one side and Loretta on the other, how could a man go wrong?

"A 'man'?" the Loretta in my head said, and fell out laughing. "Not yet hefted a Gillette and thinks he's a man!"

thirty-three

Ready or not, I biked over to the Circle of Life, my stomach wishing I hadn't drunk that lemonade. I wheeled past Draper's Used Cars and turned into the cracked parking lot. There were no customers, but I went around to the back and in the employees' door anyway.

I can still see Uncle Marty as I found him, completely deglazed, without his baker's apron, just standing by the fryer, waiting for me.

I don't want to go any further than this, to tell how he said, "Sit down, Sonny," and pulled out a stool from under the worktable. I don't want to say that his face looked beaten, so that I felt guilty and even more afraid—not for me but for him.

I'm going to say it, though. I'll never get over this if I don't.

Uncle Marty didn't sit down. He wasn't mad anymore, but he seemed to need the dignity of standing. "Sometimes the Lord puts a lot on us," he started. "And there's no way we can understand why. We know His grace is sufficient, but we don't always feel that way, Sonny. And we don't always stay on the path."

I nodded, afraid if I opened my mouth I'd say, "No sermons," and he'd order me out again.

"Your daddy—Leon—is a good man. Beautiful in every way." Oh God, I thought. This is it. "A fine daddy for a boy to take after, and you do."

Another nod. Mama often said I took after Daddy too, but she always added, "Unfortunately."

"My whole life I've been, well, *allergic* to women—"

A laugh bolted out of my mouth. I tried to stop it but that only made it sharper. "Sorry," I said.

Uncle Marty's face flushed with anger or shame or both, but he went on. "I was just about your age when I fell in love with Leon."

I wanted to scream Shut up! and run out the back door, but I made myself stay, willed my hands not to cover my ears.

"Of course, I never told him. Or anybody else, for that matter. I watched him grow up and get a job and marry Selma, and start the kind of life the Lord withheld from me. I had my faith and church and work. I gave up expecting more.

"Even in this small town, I never saw Leon much. He was busy with his job and family and he worshiped with the Methodists. Kiwanis was about the only place we met, and he didn't always attend.

"I should say here that I've always been a person people confide in. I don't know why—maybe they can tell I'm no competition. Anyway, for whatever reason, Leon stopped me one Tuesday as we were going out of the Chat 'n' Chew—Kiwanis met there then, as it does now. He put his hand on my arm"—here Uncle Marty touched his left arm as though he still knew the spot—"and said, 'Martin'—he always calls me Martin—'there's something I need to talk to you about.'

"'Oh,' I said, in shock. 'Now?'

"He said no, he had to get back to work but how about the next evening. That would be Wednesday, of course, and I had prayer meeting and choir, but I decided on the spot to skip them, which was a bad sign, Sonny. A bad sign.

"We met at my apartment. I was a nervous wreck."

Something was happening to Uncle Marty as he told this story. He seemed younger and he used his hands more when he talked.

"I cleaned everything twice. I made coffee and put out fruit—I was managing the produce section at the Piggly Wiggly then—and also got out the medicinal whiskey just in case. When the doorbell rang, I couldn't breathe."

He was acting girlie, that's what it was! My stomach twisted.

"So he came in, sat down, took the coffee, and added I'd say an eighth of a cup of Old Grand-Dad. He drank about half of it in one swallow, and it hot and bitter. I was holding on to the couch arm, unable to believe he was really there. Finally I said, 'What is it, Leon?'

"'I need your help,' he told me. 'And I need it to be a secret.'

"He's gotten caught in a bad deal, I thought. 'Are you in trouble?' I asked him.

"'Not yet,' he said, 'But if I don't change my ways, I will be.' I held up the fruit plate. He waved it away. 'You know I travel with my job?'

"I did.

"'Well, I was in New Orleans and I met some—some very *different* sort of people, and I found—' He stopped. He drank another swig of coffee.

"'You found what?' I prompted.

"He looked at his hands, touched his wedding ring, which looked too tight. 'I've been living the wrong life,' he said.

"My heart began to race. "'Wrong how?'

"'I fell in love with someone else and it's not—' He closed his eyes, took a deep breath, then opened them again. 'Martin, you *swear* you'll never tell this?'

"'I do.'

"'On the body of Jesus?'

"'Well, I don't like to—'

"'Martin, *please*.'

"'I swear.'

"'It's not a woman.'

"'Lord have mercy,' I said.

"'I hope so,' Leon said. 'Mozier won't.'"

My stomach hurt so bad now. I thought for sure I'd throw up. And I doubted that Uncle Marty would notice.

"'And I can't, I can't *live* like this, Martin, going there, being with him, returning here, pretending. But I have these children. And Selma. How can I leave them?'

"He was in anguish, Sonny."

Me too.

"And I wasn't having an easy time myself," Uncle Marty went on. "I prayed. I prayed hard to keep quiet. You haven't told him all these years, I said to myself. Don't do it now.

"'I'm sorry to burden you with this,' Leon said, 'but I have a huge favor to ask. You've always been kind to me'—my heart was starting to feel like a bruise. . . ."

And my stomach felt worse.

"'And you don't have family obligations of your own. If I find a way to leave, could you keep an eye out for Selma and my children?'"

"For you, anything, I thought. What I said was, 'Of course.'

"'And could I stay in touch with you to find out how they are?'

"I nodded, dizzy from all I was losing and gaining at once."

"Dizzy" was it. And cold, with sweat dripping off me, like that lemonade pitcher Mamby had set on the table.

"'I know it's a lot to ask,' your daddy went on. 'A life-work. But you're the only one I trust. You're so steady, and you have a good heart.'

"That was too much. I said, 'And I've loved you since we were boys.'

"Leon looked startled. 'Our friendship does go back,' he said.

"I couldn't help it. I reached over and took his hand. 'I mean what you mean,' I said."

I had my lips shut tight. My stomach lurched. Uncle Marty wasn't looking at me. He wasn't looking anywhere. His eyes had let go of focus.

"So that was it," he said.

"*What* was it?" I asked him, barely opening my mouth.

"I said if he was going, he'd better go on. And he did."

Like a fist, those words hit the bottom of my stomach, forced it inside out, shooting all that sourness up my throat and out my mouth. I didn't even have time to bend over, so Marty was hit right in the belly. He grabbed the trash can and set it in front of me and I held on to the tin rim for life. Way more came out than ever went in. I felt like I was pulling it up from my feet before it was over. One of Marty's hands was on my back and the other cupped my forehead.

When it finally stopped he gave me a damp dishrag to wipe my face with. I wanted water but he said I shouldn't drink any yet, to just go rinse out my mouth. I walked over to the tiny bathroom. When I looked in the mirror, I saw I was sort of weaving, like a tree that had grown too fast. I rinsed my face and then my mouth. I spat and spat into the dingy sink, but I could never get rid of what I knew.

When I came out, Uncle Marty had washed off his shirtfront. He'd mopped up the floor, too. "Feel better?" he asked.

"My stomach does."

"I'm almost finished," he said. I sat back down. I felt too flimsy to stand up. "That's how I came to be your guardian, Sonny. Appointed by your father and accepted by your mother, even though she never knew why. That's how I came to your house, got you to One-Way, shepherded your family. To watch you for your daddy. To help you all for him. And writing letters is part of it."

"Where is he?" I asked. My big question, and I was so used up I didn't even sound curious.

"I don't know," Uncle Marty said. "I write to him through his friends."

"Would that be Raymond and Eddie?"

Uncle Marty's eyes widened. "How do you know?"

"I *went* there," I said, "that weekend I was gone. I'd found your letter and I thought it would lead me to Daddy." And now I don't care, I thought. Why did I ever care?

"Well, I'll be," he said. "I wish you'd talked to me then."

"Why would I?" I lashed out. "You'd been hiding him and lying to us!"

"Now, Sonny," Uncle Marty said softly. "That's not fair."

"*You're* talking to me about 'fair'?" I stood up.

"But I've only *helped* you," he said, looking all at once like he might cry.

"The hell you have!" I said.

"Sonny! Watch your language!"

"My LANGUAGE?" I was mad as thunder. "I don't care about the words! I want the truth!"

"I just gave it to you."

"No. The truth is you've had Daddy all these years and we haven't."

"But that's what he—"

"And you don't want me to tell."

His face went white.

"I'm supposed to go on working for you, knowing this lie."

"What lie?" Anger roughed up his voice. "This is the truth! The truth that your daddy loved you, and Deaton, and Loretta. That he appointed a caretaker. That all these years through me he's been watching over you."

"Spying, you mean! Seeing when he can't be seen. That's not love!"

"It's what God does," Uncle Marty said.

"So God went to New Orleans and turned queer?"

"Sonny Bradshaw!" Uncle Marty exclaimed. "That's blasphemy!"

"So what? This story you've told me is not exactly a Sunday school lesson."

Uncle Marty let out his breath. "No, it's not," he agreed, all that anger sad now, heavy.

"And won't he go to Hell?"

"Who?"

"My daddy, Leon, the beautiful man you say you love. According to One-Way isn't he damned to Hell?"

"Sonny—" Uncle Marty looked at me with such pain in his face, I knew I should stop. But I couldn't.

"And what about you?"

"Stop, Sonny, stop!" Uncle Marty pleaded, tears and

sweat rolling down his cheeks. "I can't take this!" He reached behind him for something. I headed for the door. "Oh Jesus!" he cried, and covered his face with a dish towel.

thirty-four

I left him there, just like that. Still shaky, I rode straight to the Chat 'n' Chew in hopes of catching Loretta before she went home. Never mind my promises to Uncle Marty. He'd been lying. I could lie too.

The Chat 'n' Chew is right next to the barbershop, which means in summertime, with the windows open, the sidewalk in front of it smells like Aqua Velva fried chicken.

I stepped inside. Mrs. Fidge Smith, the owner, was working the cash register. "Excuse me," I said. "I'm looking for my sister, Loretta."

"*You're* polite," she said, and at first I thought that would be the extent of it, but after fluffing up the tickets on the ticket spike like they were a feather pillow, she said, "Her shift's over. She's probably out back waiting for that boy."

"Thanks," I said, stepping out onto the street again. I wheeled my bike through the narrow alley between the Chat 'n' Chew and the ten-cent store. Sure enough, Loretta was there, and she was smoking.

"Retta!" I said, just above a whisper. There was no one around, but I still felt watched.

She jumped. "Little Leon! What are you doing here?"

"I've got to talk to you," I said.

"Then spill. Wesley will be here any minute."

"I don't *care* about Wesley," I started.

"Good," Loretta cut in.

I couldn't believe she'd said that. "Loretta, I've just found out our Daddy is . . . is . . . ."

"Miss America!"

"Loretta!" Her being ridiculous and right at the same time made my eyes hurt. I leaned forward and said near her ear, "He's a queer."

She pulled back. "You smell awful!"

"Did you hear me?"

"Of course I heard you," Retta said, taking a quick pull on her cigarette. "You think that's news?"

I was stunned. "How did you know?"

"I'm alive and I pay attention."

"So do I!" I protested.

She sighed wearily. "Yes, but you pay attention to what you're thinking and feeling. I pay attention to what's going on. And," she said, pausing for a deep drag this time, then exhaling plumes over her shoulder, "I eavesdrop."

"You do?"

"How else am I going to survive in a family tight-lipped as tombs?"

"They talk all the time," I said.

"Sure," she said. "About butter beans and bowel trouble and how we ought to behave, but about *real* stuff, like the fact that our daddy waltzed off one day and never came back, not a word. Not to us. So I had to listen in."

"Does Mama know?" I asked.

"Mama doesn't *want* to know," Loretta said. "Being a cast-off woman is bad enough, but being cast off for a man? She'd be dust in the road."

"How about Aunt Joy?"

"Don't know and don't care." Loretta said impatiently. "It was Hickman and Sink I heard talking about it."

"But Uncle Sink's mean," I reminded her. "How did you know he wasn't making it up?"

"Because I'd heard rumors, bits of things at school, only I hadn't known what they meant."

"Like what?" I asked, just as I heard the Harley roar into range and begin its crescendo toward us. Loretta took one last puff and threw the nub of her cigarette down, massaging it into the gravel with her shoe.

"Tell Mama I'm out with Wesley," she ordered.

"But Loretta, I'm not—"

Wesley pulled up, loud and gleaming. Retta hiked her orange skirt and threw her leg over the motorcycle seat. She hooked one arm around Wesley's middle and with the other gave me a wave. "Welcome to the world, Sonny!" she called, and they were off.

thirty-five

I went home, and told Mama about Loretta. She fussed and fumed and I said "Yes" and "No." The same with Deaton. He had a scheme to put on a circus, with Cantaloupe jumping through Grandma's quilting hoop. He could make his fortune in nickel admissions. I just said "Okay" and "Sure" and "You ought to think more about that." I could NOT think about it. I could not think about anything, least of all the scene I'd just had with Marty. My head hurt, my stomach felt all pinched up, and my heart was pumping dread instead of blood.

"I don't feel so hot," I told Mama and Deaton, and went and lay down on my bed.

The Loretta in my head said I was being ridiculous. How had she put it? "You pay attention to what you're

thinking and feeling. I pay attention to what's going on."
So what *was* going on?

I had found a secret and told it—not to the world but to one of the people who was keeping it.

So what was so bad about that?

Nothing, I told myself. Uncle Marty really *is* in touch with Daddy. He's admitted being sent to spy. All I've done is tell a guilty person I know the truth.

Then why do I feel sick?

Would Loretta feel sick?

She'd laugh at me wondering.

But I *do* wonder. I thought I'd feel better and I don't. I feel worse. That must mean something.

For starters, I'd heard more than I wanted to know— about Daddy and Uncle Marty both. Ugh.

I looked up through the grid of springs at the mattress on Deaton's bunk. Dull, dumb, stuck, just like me. I wanted to tear it—tear something—apart. I punched it with my fist. That just hurt my knuckles. I jabbed it with my foot. The mattress jumped a little. Then I bent my knees and began stomping it with my upside-down feet. The pillow flew off, followed by Deaton's stuffed snake. Then there was a crash—something plastic had hit the floor—and Mama hollered, "What's going on in there?"

"Nothing," I said, rolling over on my side and getting out of the bunk. "I'm just thinking."

"Well, don't break anything," she said.

What had fallen was the camera, Mama's precious Kodak. (What was Deaton doing with that?) But what had landed was this fact: I felt bad because of Mama. If I told her the truth, something in her would break. A lot of her life was built on Uncle Marty being part of our family because he loved us, and if I told . . . so I had found out this truth and now I was stuck with it.

"Shit!" I said under my breath. "Goddamned gift-wrapped shit!" That was Uncle Sink's expression, and now I knew what it meant. You think you know something—like what you're doing—and you don't. You go for something good, but when you get it, it's not pure like you thought. It stinks in that really serious way and you're the one who unwrapped it, you're the one who's holding it, trailing ribbons and colored paper.

"Sonny," Loretta said, Loretta who had pressed the thumb of her voice deep into my mind. "Flush."

But Loretta—

"Let it go. Turn off the twenty-watt bulb of your brain and go to sleep."

Right, I said. And after counting backward from a hundred to about fourteen, I did.

thirty-six

Then it was morning. And what was I going to do—go to work? Deaton was asleep above me, snoring his toy snore. I'll go back to sleep, I thought. And if Mama wakes me up, I'll say I'm sick.

That might have worked, except my eyelids were like an overwound shade. Every time I got them down they sprang back up again. I stared at Deaton's mattress and considered kicking it some more, with him on it. He'd wake up in a panic, thinking we were having an earthquake.

Mama would never believe I was sick if I did that. And I wasn't sick, that was the problem. No, the problem was that I had to go back to the Circle of Life. What could I say to Uncle Marty? What would he say to me? My stomach felt like a baseball mitt someone just socked their fist into. I might as well go on and get it over with, I thought. Having to face him next time he came over to dinner would be worse.

I got up. I looked at my feet. They were so dumb. They had no idea what was going on.

When I got dressed and got to the kitchen Mamby was just coming in the back door. As always she had a worn paper sack with her, and she turned on the oven for biscuits as she went by. "That's my working shoes," she'd told me years ago when I'd asked her what was in the sack. "I've got my walking shoes and my working shoes."

She sat down at the table to change.

"Morning, Sonny," she said.

"Morning, Mamby."

Having just been thinking about my own feet, I looked at Mamby's as she unlaced her tennis shoes and put on black leather ones. Her feet were small for someone as big as she was, and they were sort of knotted. She saw me looking.

"Got stories, these feet," she said.

"They do?"

"Read them in other people's shoes," she said.

I thought for a minute. "You mean handed-down shoes like when I wear Albion's and then Deaton gets what's left?"

"No," Mamby said. "My feet wear shoes that were broke in further back than that. And they don't know who did it." She gave a joyless laugh. "Might have been some white lady."

She put her walking shoes in the sack and set it in the broom closet. Then she washed her hands, put on her apron, and got out the biscuit bowl.

"How's your mama this morning?"

"I don't know. I haven't seen her." Just then I heard the shower go on. "There she is," I said.

"Humph!" Mamby said. "Getting up late. She'll be down in the mouth."

"Yeah. I think I'll just eat some cornflakes and go on to work."

"Suit yourself," Mamby said.

Had I hurt her feelings? I looked at her. She was working lard into flour with her fingers. Wasn't she going to tell me hot biscuits make a better start to the day than cold cereal? Then I thought, Well, if you can remember that, maybe it's time for you to say it to yourself. But I didn't. I was out the door before the biscuits were out of the oven.

The Circle of Life was crowded when I got there—all six tables full and three or four people at the window. Marty was too busy to say anything to me. I just went in the kitchen and set to washing trays and icing ladles and the dowel rods he uses to flip donuts when they're frying.

This is good, I told myself. We can just settle into our work, and let our tempers settle too.

When rush hour was over he came and stood beside me like he was waiting for something. He didn't speak.

Finally I took a deep breath and, looking at a Texas-shaped grease spot on his apron, said, "For Mama's sake I'm not going to tell."

Uncle Marty let out a huge sigh. "Thank the Lord! The last thing I want is to hurt Selma. Oh, Sonny, you've got a real heart! You are Leon's boy." Uncle Marty looked like he might cry.

I'm doing this because I'm *Selma's* boy, I thought, but I didn't say that. The less I said, the less trouble I could get myself into.

Uncle Marty reached out to pat me on the shoulder, but then stopped his hand about an inch away. It made me think of when the icing cracks on a cake donut and falls off and then you can't sell it. I felt rotten.

Business was good that day, though, and I worked hard to keep up with all the dirty dishes it takes to feed a few people who want stuff sticky with sugar and crispy with grease.

About two thirty, when everyone had cleared out, Uncle Marty came over to where I was mixing up the next day's glaze.

"Sonny," he said, "you've worked nonstop since you got here. I'll bet you didn't even have lunch."

"No time," I said.

"Why don't you quit early then? Just take off now and go have lunch at home."

"But we need more chocolate icing. I've got the chocolate melting," I said, pointing to the hot-plate sort of thing with the copper pot that we used just for that.

"I'll take care of it," he said. "This heat is merciless, and you know I promised your mother not to overwork you. . . ."

"Okay," I said, my voice wavery. The sooner I got out the better, but I didn't like the way Marty was looking at me. His face was red as a stove eye turned on high.

Still, I took my apron off and put it in the laundry bag, washed my hands, and then dried them on the only dry cloth left.

"Tell Selma I'll let her know if I'm coming to supper," Uncle Marty said as I headed for the door.

Was this a test? I wondered. Did he expect me to object?

But I just said, "Sure," and left and didn't look back.

As I pedaled through the moist heavy air I thought how good a really big thunderstorm would feel, but I checked the sky and it didn't look likely.

When I got home, I heard singing above the crunch of the gravel as I rode down the driveway. It wasn't Mamby, though. It was the radio! How strange. Mama wasn't home—no car—and it was early yet for Loretta. Could Mamby be playing the radio?

As I came in the back door, she put down the iron and reached over to where the red radio sat by the toaster and switched the music off. "Just hunting the news," she said.

"News?"

"Lot going on," she said.

"Like what?"

"How about you?" she answered. "How come you're home so early?"

"Uncle Marty thinks it's too hot," I told her, opening the Frigidaire and taking out the big jar of sweet tea. She'd put mint in it too. I love mint, even though it grows beside the garage on the way to the whipping place.

Mamby went back to ironing. I poured some tea in one of Mama's iridescent aluminum tumblers—the green one—and sat down at the table.

"Yes sir, it's hot," Mamby said, and picked up the sprinkler bottle to shake a little water onto the pants she had on the board. "Great day for ironing."

I nodded and drank the tea straight down.

"Sonny, do me a favor," Mamby said when I got up to set the tumbler in the sink. "Go bring in that last load off the line."

"Sure," I said. I grabbed the basket from the floor beside the stove and went out the screen door. I didn't think the backyard could be hotter than the house, but standing under the clothesline I felt like a hamburger on the grill.

thirty-seven

I think we had just started on dessert when we heard the siren. Mama had given up on Uncle Marty, who hadn't called. I think we were looking at cherry Jell-O and tapioca parfait Mama'd set down before us, and she said, "Lord help the suffering," like she always did when that wail started. Then we ate up red wobbles and glue and forgot all about it until a little while later, when Mrs. Jackson came to the door—the front door, which she never does. "Would you get your mother, please, Sonny?" she said when I answered the bell. She smelled like fish.

Mama came to the door, massaging lotion into her hands. "Won't you come in?" she asked. The front door made her formal.

Mrs. Jackson shook her head. "There's been a fire at

the donut shop," she said. "Muriel"—that was her married daughter—"just called. I thought you'd want to know."

Mama opened the screen door and we went out onto the porch. "Oh, dear," she said. "I hope Marty has insurance."

"Mr. Bonner—," Mrs. Jackson started, but then turned her head to the sound of a car coming down the street. She was clearly hoping for something, and she got it. "That's your brother's car, isn't it?" she said to Mama.

"I believe you're right," Mama replied.

"I'll be going then," Mrs. Jackson said.

She's acting strange, I thought. But then she's always a little strange. She's the woman who put a bathtub full of dirt in the backyard so she didn't have to bend over so far to plant onions.

Uncle Sink pulled up in the driveway, the maroon and white of his Bel Air glowing in the fading light. If the fire's bad enough, I thought, maybe I won't have to go to work tomorrow.

Uncle Sink got out, and then the passenger door opened too. I thought it might be Albion, but it was Aunt Joy. By the time they got to the porch, Mrs. Jackson had disappeared around the gardenia bush.

"You heard, Sis?" Uncle Sink asked as he came up the steps. It couldn't be too bad if he was calling her "Sis."

"Oh, Selma," Aunt Joy said, taking Mama's hands, lotion and all.

"How bad is it?" Mama asked.

"Sit her down," Uncle Sink commanded.

I went stone cold. They walked past me to the glider.

"Is it all gone?" Mama asked, her voice all at once like a child's. "Poor Marty."

"Marty is—"

"Sinclair!" Aunt Joy cut in. "Let me do this!"

Mama was sitting in the glider now, with Aunt Joy next to her, still holding her hands. Uncle Sink was standing, looming over them. I was invisible.

"It's Marty," Aunt Joy began in a voice soft as feathers. And my heart started pounding: *oh-no, oh-no, oh-no.* "The Circle of Life caught fire and either he was already in there or he ran in hoping to put it out."

"No!" Mama cried, and tried to get up. Aunt Joy's arm went around her shoulder and Uncle Sink stationed himself on the other side.

"Selma," Aunt Joy said. There were tears in her voice. "Selma, honey—"

Just then another car turned the corner. It was Pastor Biggs's Studebaker, and it pulled up at the curb, black and shiny. I *knew* then, sure as if Pastor Biggs had said it, as if Aunt Joy had got her words out, or Uncle Sink, or Mrs. Jackson. He was dead. Burned up in the Circle of Life.

"It was the copper bowl," I said. "The chocolate."

"What the—," some man said, but his words started to sparkle. Another siren yeowled, only it was Mama, her voice huge, glittery. I got caught in the swirls, like water, like flame. Then it all went black.

thirty-eight

I woke up in the bottom bunk, with Deaton's hand dangling over the side of the top. It was grubby, which seemed strange—Mama never let us get into bed without a bath. "I respect my sheets," she'd say. But there was Deaton's paw, almost sooty. Too black for our dirt, I thought—we have sand. And then, That's not dirt, that's ashes.

Uncle Marty—oh my God, it couldn't, *couldn't* have happened. Last night was just a nightmare. In a minute I'd get up and get dressed and eat biscuits and honey and before long I'd be back at the Circle of Life. "Yea, though I walk through the valley of the shadow of death . . ." No, I wouldn't think like that. I'd think of trays with chocolate icing rings waiting for soap and water, of the griddle to scrape, the used oil to strain. "That's a dangerous job," Uncle Marty had told me. "Never let it spill. Oil on the floor can lead to falls, which can lead to burns or concussions. Oil spilled on a burner or pilot light can burst into flame. And never leave the burner on under the copper bowl."

Was that what happened? Had Uncle Marty forgotten it? Melting chocolate was my job, but he'd sent me home early. And I was happy to go. I had fled. "Whither shall I go from thy spirit?" Stop it, Sonny. No Scripture. But that's what he'd said to me yesterday: "Stop, Sonny, stop! I can't take this!"

I pulled the sheet over my head. This couldn't be happening. But the feel of the white cloth on my nose and mouth made me think of Uncle Marty and the dish towel and of the sheet you pull up over the dead. "If I make the grave my bed, you are there."

I was maybe the last person who saw him alive. . . . That gave me the shivers, even on a hot Alabama morning.

One knock on the door and someone pushed it open. "Out of your holes, you muskrats!" Loretta called. "Mama's orders."

When did Loretta get home? I wondered. Who told her?

Thump! Deaton never bothered with the ladder. There he stood in my old sailboat pajamas. They were too little for him, but he wouldn't give them up.

"Sonny," he said, rubbing his eyes. "You all right?"

"I'm fine," I said.

"Uncle Sink and Pastor Biggs laid you on the front walk and dumped a bucket of water on you."

"Like I was on fire," I said.

"Do you remember?"

"No."

"Uncle Marty—"

"Oh, I remember that."

"And Mama fainted and fell and broke her wrist and that girl from up the street came down to help," Deaton said all in one breath.

"The girl who just moved in?"

"Um-hmm. She was walking her dog when Mama fell over, and even with all the commotion, including you, we could hear Mama's bone crack, and Nell— that's her name—just tied her dog to the porch rail and said, 'What can I do?' She has a *tall* dog named Tolliver and I think she likes emergencies. She got Mama up and—"

"Deaton!" It was Sergeant Loretta again.

"And then Uncle Sink took us to the fire—I mean, to what was left—"

"Now!" she commanded. "Stop running at the mouth and get dressed!"

It was only the three of us at the breakfast table.

Mamby served biscuits and fried apples, her face squinched like a morning glory at night. "Oh, children," she said when she set down the juice, then said it again with the butter. And with the honey, "Bless these poor hearts."

"Where's Mama?" I asked.

"With the undertaker," Loretta said. She was wearing a canvas dress covered with blue lines like highways on a map. It tied on like it wasn't really clothes.

"Undertaker?" Deaton echoed.

I rushed to say, "At the funeral home," but that didn't distract Loretta.

"He's the guy who pumps the blood out of dead people and then pumps in other stuff to keep them nice and fresh till they're planted."

"Planted?" Deaton echoed again.

"Buried. The undertaker takes them under."

"You mean Uncle Marty?" Deaton asked.

"Well," Loretta said, then paused to swallow her bite of biscuit. "If there's enough left of—"

"Hush now," Mamby said, turning around from the sink. "You got to show the dead some respect."

Loretta sat up straight. "I was just *educating*—"

"No, honey. That was mocking," Mamby said. Loretta scowled.

"Uncle Marty is dead like *that*?" Deaton asked.

I was waiting for a hoot and a great line from Loretta, but they didn't come.

Mamby walked around to Deaton's chair. She put her hand on his shoulder. "Your Uncle Marty's fine," she said. "He's gone to be with his Lord, and he's just fine."

thirty-nine

After breakfast Mamby had us clean up our rooms. "A lot of folks going to be in and out," she said.

"Who?" I asked, just as Deaton said, "What for?"

"Church folks bringing food and other Mozier folks who knew Mr. Bonner."

"But why are they coming here?" I asked.

"You're his family," Mamby said. "Now run on."

"They're not coming in our *room*," Deaton insisted.

"People get in a house, they might go anywhere," Mamby said.

So we made up our beds and picked up our clothes and hid our junk. Deaton wanted to leave his burnt match collection out—he had taken them out of ashtrays when smokers visited and saved them in a mayonnaise jar—but I thought under the circumstances he ought not.

"*We're* not Uncle Marty's family," Deaton complained, hunting for a place on the closet floor to put his jar. It was crowded with his shoes, my shoes, balls, bats, roller skates. . . .

"We're what he had," I said, thinking, If only you knew: Daddy gave us to him.

"What happened to his real people?" Deaton asked.

"I don't know," I said, trying to get my sock-and-underwear drawer closed. The front had come unglued on one side, so the whole thing was crooked. "Maybe he didn't have many relatives and those died off."

"I'll ask Mama," he said.

"Not—" But the doorbell rang and Deaton exclaimed, "Food!" and ran to answer it.

It wasn't food. It was Nell Kivitt. She'd come to see how Mama's wrist was. Turns out she had splinted it with some scraps of Masonite she found in the garage. She was probably checking up on me, too, since she was there when I keeled over.

Of course, we didn't *know* how Mama was. We hadn't seen her that morning and we hadn't asked. "Let's ask Mamby," I said. "Come on back."

Nell followed me, all shining in white pants and shirt. She'd tied the tails of the shirt in front so a little of her skinny middle showed. It was amazing.

Until we got to the kitchen door, I wasn't thinking how Nell had been there at night and not met Mamby. I was thinking how Uncle Marty was all of a sudden out of our lives and this stranger was in. It didn't make sense.

Mamby was mopping the floor, so we stopped at the doorsill.

"Mamby," I said, and she stood straight. "This is Nell Kivitt, who moved in down the street. She helped Mama last night and wants to know how her wrist is."

"The doctor said both bones was broke, but it was clean and ought to heal right up."

"Good," Nell said.

"Quicker than her heart," Mamby added, and started mopping again.

"Thank you," Nell said, and we went back down the hall. Deaton had disappeared. I walked her to the door and opened it, but when she went out onto the porch she didn't leave, so I went out too.

"You have a *colored* servant?" she said, and it was more of an accusation than a question.

"She works for us," I said.

Nell ruffled her hair, short and shiny as new grass. "I've heard about the South," she said. "But I didn't believe it."

I bit my tongue and said, "You just got here. If you knew us, you'd see Mamby's like family."

"Really?" She took a deep, superior breath.

"Look," I said. "I can't talk now. Our friend has died." Then, because I could be rude too, I said, "Where's your mother?"

Nell let the breath out. "Dead."

"I'm sorry."

"And where's your father?" she asked.

"Nobody knows," I told her. "He walked out when Deaton was a baby. Uncle Marty tried to be a daddy to us."

"The donut shop man?" I nodded. "With all the Bible verses on the menu?"

"I painted that sign," I told her. "I worked for him." And I started to say what I just this minute remembered: He was the closest thing to a daddy Deaton ever knew. "Excuse me," I said. "I've got to find Deaton."

"I'll be back," Nell said.

forty

Deaton was on his bed under his bathrobe.

"What's wrong with you?"

"They'll just bring casseroles," he said from under the cloth.

"Oh, no," I told him. "Somebody will bring cake."

"But no more donuts," he said in a real small voice.

I climbed the ladder and sat beside him. I wanted to put my hand on his back but I felt stupid. "Maybe in Heaven," I said.

"I don't want to wait till Heaven for donuts!"

"When Daddy walked out I hated everybody," I said.

"Even me?" Deaton asked.

"No, not you. You can't hate babies."

"Daddy did."

"He did not."

"How do you know?"

"Look, Deaton. I don't think when Daddy left it had anything to do with us."

Silence. Then Deaton said, "I don't want those matches anymore."

"Okay."

"Let's throw them in the creek."

"Okay."

He sat up. The gray-striped bathrobe slid off his splotchy red face. "Right now," he said.

"No. We'll get all dirty and snagged up if we go through the brambles, and those people are coming."

"Sonny, you are turning into a grown-up," Deaton said, disgusted.

"Sorry. How about we bury the jar?"

"Right now?"

"If that's what you want."

So in a few minutes we were out behind the garage with the jar of burnt matches and a shovel. We took turns digging. When the hole was big enough, Deaton pulled some grass from around it and covered the bottom before he laid the jar in.

"Now pray."

"Come on, Deaton!"

"When you bury something, you pray," he insisted.

"Oh, all right." I bowed my head. "God is great, God is good—"

"Sonny!"

"That's just what came into my mind."

"Well, look for something else," he said.

I bowed my head again. I breathed in that smell of garage wood and motor oil I connected with the lash of Uncle Sink's belt. The grace he prayed had the same beat as his whippings: "Good food, good meat. Good God, let's eat!" But I didn't say that. I opened my mouth, and what came out was "Lord, let what we bury rest in peace." And my skin remembered something else—the invisible hand on the back of my neck when Uncle Marty prayed at One-Way.

"And help Mama," I said. "Amen."

"Amen," answered Deaton. He pulled some chicory from a clump next to the garbage can and dropped the blue blooms on top of the jar.

"You want to fill it in?" I asked. He reached for the shovel.

When that was done he said, "We've got to sing."

"Enough is enough!" I said. "I am not singing over a jar." Deaton made his mad face, but his lower lip trembled, and I gave in. "Something short," I said. He nodded. I couldn't think of a funeral song, so I just picked one I knew Deaton knew:

He's the lily of the valley.
He's the bright and morning star.
He's the fairest of ten thousand.
Everybody ought to know.

forty-one

By noon the kitchen looked like One-Way's does right before they have a Fellowship Dinner. The Frigidaire was so packed you couldn't have put a mouse in there. Ham and potato salad, combination salad, broccoli casserole, green beans and new potatoes, roast beef, pickled beets, deviled eggs, coleslaw. And the counter was a row of desserts: upside-down cake, cherry pie, coconut-cashew bars, and peach buckle. There was even a chocolate whipped cream thing called Snow on the Mountain balanced in the Frigidaire on top of the green beans.

I know all this because I was the scribe, writing down everything that came in, who brought it, and what kind of dish it was in so that, later on, Mama could get the thank-you notes and container returns right. Deaton knew it too, because he looked under every piece of tinfoil and every Tupperware lid.

Mama came home about twelve thirty, right after the pie arrived. The bright white cast from just above her fingers to right below her elbow was the only solid thing about her. The rest looked like a tent that's collapsed and been propped back up wrong. She came in slowly, sat at the kitchen table, moved a salt shaker, and said, "The funeral will be at two tomorrow."

I tried to think of something to say. Mamby was in the backyard hanging out the fancy tablecloth she'd washed. "You want some sweet tea?" I asked. Mama shook her head. "A sandwich?"

She put both elbows on the table and leaned forward, her face in her hands. "Coffee," she said.

"How do I make it?"

Any other time she would have jumped up and done it, but this day she told me step by step. I spilled almost a whole scoop getting it out of the canister. It felt like paper dirt.

"Where's your sister?" Mama asked.

"At work, I guess. She disappeared after breakfast."

"She shouldn't *be* at work," Mama said. "Not when the family's in mourning. And there's supposed to be a wreath on the door. Where's the wreath?"

I shrugged.

"What about Deaton?"

"In the backyard," I said. I didn't tell her he was decorating the grave of a mayonnaise jar.

"Sonny," Mama said, as the coffee gurgled and *pripped* into the little glass dome of the percolator, "Mamby said you went back to help Uncle Marty late yesterday. Did he seem all right then?"

"Yes," I said, my heart lurching to full throttle like Wesley's motorcycle.

"It's not like him to be careless. He knew his business, what was safe and what was not—" Her voice got pinched. Don't cry! Please! I thought, and she didn't. She went on, "I can't see how this happened."

"A kitchen is a dangerous place," I said. "He told me that."

Mama nodded. And then, as if I'd asked, she said, "It's in all the papers: Mozier, Andalusia, Mobile."

"Mobile?"

The screen door hinges creaked as Mamby came in. Deaton was right behind her. His voice, which had been solemn all day, was bubbly now. "Cantaloupe got my pajama top out of the laundry basket. She dragged it over to the bush just like she'd killed something." His open face waited for delight, but there wasn't any. "Mama," he said.

She held out her good arm and Deaton ran to her for

a hug. It made my chest hurt. You get as big as me and you don't *get* hugs.

"Selma," Mamby said, going to the stove and turning down the heat because coffee was leaping out of the spout. "You look like I feel."

Then it seemed like Silence, real as a person, came in the room and stood there with us and we were all hushed and stopped till it left.

"Would you sit down and have some coffee?" Mama asked Mamby. "Sonny made it."

"Look out!" Deaton said.

Mamby poured the coffee and took the chair opposite me. I wanted to leave and I didn't want to leave. Deaton was stuck to Mama. "I'm hungry," he said.

"I made up a plate of sandwiches," Mamby told him. "Sonny, would you reach those to me? They're on the middle shelf."

I had to move three things to get the big plate out. Mamby set it in the middle of the table. "You want milk?" I asked Deaton.

"Lemonade," he said. So I poured him some. *I* didn't want any, that was for sure. I didn't think I'd ever drink lemonade again.

There were napkins on the table. We used them for plates.

"How is Nissa?" Mama asked.

"Not speaking," Mamby told her. "Not to me or her daddy or Freelan. So I don't know how she is except stubborn."

"Will she try the leg?" Mama asked.

Mamby shook her head. "Won't hardly use the crutches."

"Will she eat?" Deaton asked.

"She only wants ice cream," Mamby said. Deaton grinned. That was his favorite food in the world. "And she can't have that."

"Why not?" Deaton asked.

"Sugar," Mamby told him. "She's got too much sugar."

"Why—?" Deaton started, but Mama gave him a look and shook her head.

I took a bite of my ham sandwich. It was as good as it could be: soft white bread, a little mayonnaise and mustard, ham salty and sweet. It tasted awful.

"Last night, Mr. Bill"—I don't know why she calls her husband Mr. Bill—"said to Nissa—and that man hasn't put more than ten words together at a time in twenty years—he said, 'Nissa, God done give you what He give you and you got to accept it. It's your life, ain't nothing more precious. But sometimes you got to fight for it.' And he pulled up his shirt and showed her the scar where he got scalded when a boiler cap blew and the steam hit him.

It's bigger than this," Mamby said, touching the gold rim of the plate that held the sandwiches, "and he's always hid it from the children, afraid it might scare them. 'Happened before you was born,' he said. 'I was on a run up to Baltimore. Wound up in a hospital in Virginia. Couldn't no kin get to me. Pain like hellfire. Doctors afraid some of my insides might be cooked. None of my plumbing worked either,' he said. 'And I thought, This is wrong. This is the awfullest thing. I didn't do nothing to deserve being scalded like a chicken but not yet killed. I got a wife and a baby coming. I can't work, might never work. Lie around, be somebody's burden. I'm *useless.* God has throwed me away.'

"'Then what?' Nissa asked.

"'I commenced to die,' Mr. Bill told her. 'Wouldn't open my mouth. Wouldn't swallow what water they could get in me. 'Course, they had their needles, but everything they shot in just leaked out the burns.'

"'Then what?' Nissa asked again.

"'Then I looked at my hand,' her daddy said. 'This big powerful hand'—he held it up—'that had got so poor and feeble. And in my mind—no, it was in my heart; in my heart I saw my daddy's hand, work-wore and callused with a thick scar across the palm that I didn't even know where he got, and it went through me like lightning; I don't *know* what he suffered. And his daddy, Zekiel, he was born a

SLAVE, so what am I doing here, about to give up and die in a *hospital?* Their hands is in these hands'—he held his out, then reached over and took ahold of Nissa's. 'They held on to life—and it bitter, sweet, scalded, and maimed—they didn't let go. So I didn't. And you won't either. You got these *hands.*'" Mamby sat back in her chair. Tears rolled down her cheeks. "And you know what that girl said? She looked at her daddy, who'd just give her his heart on a plate, and she said, 'But I can't walk.' 'You can if you will,' he told her."

Mama was crying too, but she wasn't quiet about it. Tears poured out of her puffy eyes and hiccupy sounds came from her throat like a little engine about to sputter out.

"Can I see that scar?" Deaton asked Mamby.

Mama blotted her face with a napkin, put that in her broken hand, then reached over with the other to touch Mamby's arm where it rested on the table. "Thank you," she said.

forty-two

That night was the Visitation, which is where the family has to go to the funeral home and stand by the coffin so other people can come and hug them or shake their hands and say how sorry they are that the person who is in the coffin died.

Usually, at least in Mozier, the top of the coffin is open so that you have to LOOK at the body and hear everybody say the person looks natural, just like they're asleep. I remember this from when Grandpa died. Sometimes people even touch the body or put things in its hands. Mama said that when Mrs. Jackson's sister died, Mrs. Jackson wanted to put a deck of cards in with her because Heaven would be just so much sawdust to Tempa if she couldn't play Bridge.

We were spared those goings-on, though, because they didn't open Uncle Marty. We just stood by the shiny gray coffin with its handles like fancy toilet-paper holders and said "Yes" and "No" and "Thank you" and breathed whatever breaths came by: mint, onion, tobacco, whiskey, and bad.

Mama "bore up," as they say. Aunt Joy stood by her, with me and Loretta on the other side. Deaton was there too, but he could only stand the line for ten minutes. After that he sat in the folding chairs with people who'd already paid their respects or he hopped up to check out the bathroom and the water fountain. Grandma's ulcer was acting up, so she stayed home, with Aunt Roo tending to her. Uncle Hickman was out on the porch, smoking and greeting people, while Uncle Sink was under somebody's house trying to clear out their line.

Our line went on forever, and Loretta didn't say *one* thing to brighten it up. Mama had warned her before we left the house: "This is a sacred occasion and if you care even a fly swat for me, you'll hold your tongue." So she did. But several times I saw her open her mouth and close it with a little snap like a dog.

Halfway through, I asked Mama why Mamby wasn't there, and she said I knew good and well why, which of course I did by then, but I just didn't *get* it. How could Mama and Mamby cry together at the table at noon and then a little later we go downtown to a different place and

Mamby can't even come in the door? How can your heart be wide open to somebody one minute and then be closed like a . . . like a coffin?

Well, maybe Mamby couldn't have come anyway. Maybe she had to be home with Nissa and her other kids and Mr. Bill, who was the best preacher I ever heard, even though I wasn't there to hear him.

The One-Way preacher *did* show up, of course, along with Mrs. Pastor Biggs and her sister Flora, who lived with them because she wasn't quite right. When they came through the line Pastor Biggs took Mama's good hand and said, "Everything is set for the service, Sister Bradshaw, just the way we talked about. Sister Clemons has worked up the music and I've written my message, and—"

"And I've arranged the gladiolas," Mrs. Pastor Biggs put in.

"They should be *sad*iolas," Loretta whispered.

"So all is in readiness to send Elder Bonner home."

"Thank you," Mama said, sniffing a little. She had a handkerchief tucked in her cast in case she needed it.

"'My tears have been my food day and night,'" Mrs. Pastor Biggs said, quoting Scripture, and standing too close. Her breath smelled like old shoes.

"Yes," Mama said.

"But," Pastor Biggs intoned, "'He shall wipe every tear from our eyes.'"

His own eyes were halfway closed, but they shot open when Flora, who was shaped like an ironing board, said real loud, "Did the man in there commit sideways?"

"Hush!" her sister said, as a voice from the folding chairs asked, "What?"

"Sideways," Flora repeated. "You know, like when you wet leather shoelaces and tie them tight around your neck so they can choke you to death while you sleep."

"Oh, God," Mama said, and Mrs. Jackson, who was sitting with Deaton, rushed up with smelling salts. Mama waved them away, but I got a whiff. It was like having a screwdriver up your nose. "Thank you," Mama told her, "but I'm not feeling faint."

"Is it true?" Mrs. Aiken asked from the front row.

Mama bit her lip.

But Loretta, in a voice loud enough for everyone to hear, said, "The Lord knows, Mrs. Aiken. We don't."

And that was that. Nobody else said a word about it. Mama reached behind me and gave Loretta's shoulder a squeeze.

So we got through the eternity from six till eight. Then after all the callers had left and it was just us and Mr. Wilt, the undertaker, Mama said she'd like to have a few minutes alone with Uncle Marty to say good-bye.

"You want me to open him, Selma?" Mr. Wilt asked. "I'll be glad to. He looked like the devil when he came in, but I—"

"No thank you, Mr. Wilt," Mama said. "I saw him yesterday." Her voice broke there, but she put it back together. "I just want some time with him like he is."

Mr. Wilt nodded, looking disappointed.

"We'll take the children home," Aunt Joy told Mama. "And Sink will return and wait for you."

Mama gave her a kiss on the cheek. Then she turned back to the coffin room.

Deaton began to wail as we started down the hall. "I don't want to leave Mama!"

I thought, You're just leaving her for an hour. She's leaving Uncle Marty forever. Loretta said, "King Baby! I crown thee Deaton the First."

forty-three

That night I had a nightmare. Deaton and I were playing hide 'n' seek at One-Way, and he had hidden in the cubby under the podium. Loretta and Mama were downstairs cooking in the Fellowship Hall. I got distracted from the game by a songbook called *Praise Anyway*, and I was trying to read a hymn made out of lace when something moved around my waist and I looked down to see a black snake floating on muddy water. The Conecuh had flooded, and it was coming up fast.

Offering plates and communion trays with slots for thimble cups floated by. "Deaton!" I yelled. "It's a flood. Come out!" And I tried to escape the row of chairs and go up to where he was. But the water was twice as heavy as real water and I barely moved forward while it climbed up my chest. "Get out, Deaton!" I hollered, and then I realized if the water was like this up here, it was an aquarium downstairs. That's what I saw in my dream: Mama and Loretta swimming around in the Fellowship Hall, trying to get to the surface but there was no surface, bumping the ceiling, then diving down again, their dresses streaming like bright fins. "The stairs!" I yelled. "Swim to the stairs!"

Water was up to my neck. I was only halfway to the podium. I could see now there was something on top of it. Maybe the snake? But no, it stood and stretched. It was Cantaloupe. "Deaton," I yelled again. "Save your cat!" But instead of Deaton surfacing, Cantaloupe jumped in the brown water and disappeared.

I woke up seasick and so scared I had to make sure they were all okay. I got out of bed and reached up in the dark to touch Deaton's back. He was sweating and breathing. I tiptoed out of our room and down the hall to Loretta's and eased her door open. The night was hot as the fry room and Retta was out from under the covers, but she was wearing Wesley's motorcycle jacket over her nightgown.

"Sonny!" I jumped and turned around. Mama hovered in the hall like a ghost in her white nightgown. "What are you doing?"

"I had a bad dream," I told her. "I wanted to make sure everybody was all right."

"Come out to the kitchen."

"Why are *you* up?" I asked once we got into the light. She didn't sit down but went over to the back door, which was open. A tiny breeze came through the screen, and brought the smell of river with it.

"Can't sleep," she said. "I was just getting some water."

I looked at the glass on the counter, remembering what Loretta said about gin in the Get-Set bottle.

The house was so still.

I kept seeing Deaton, trapped in that little space, waiting for me to find him. I started to shake.

"Mama," I began, "if you had a really big secret and it had to do with people you knew and one of them found out about it and told you, how bad would that be?"

"What are you talking about, Sonny?" Irritation, maybe anger, pinched her voice, and she reached for her glass. She looked so pale, worn-out, old. Mama doesn't *want* to know, Loretta had said.

"Nothing," I said. "It was just the dream."

"Oh," Mama said, her voice relaxing. "I know what you mean. They can be real as day. And then—" She paused, sighed. "Sometimes you wish the *day* was a dream."

I nodded.

"Why don't I make you some chocolate milk? And then you need to go back to bed. We have another hard day tomorrow."

"Thanks," I said.

Mama bustled around getting milk, chocolate syrup, spoon. Every action seemed momentous, like she was discovering something. But maybe that was me, not her. Maybe I was seeing how relieved she was to do this familiar thing and how it helped to seal off the truth I wasn't going to tell. How fixing chocolate milk protected her view of the world.

"You're a good boy, Sonny," she said, handing me the glass. "And you've not had an easy time. I'm sorry for that."

"It's okay, Mama," I said, but I wasn't sure what she meant. Daddy leaving? The spells? Uncle Marty?

"Your daddy said you were smart as two people and that alone would give you a rough road. And Marty"—she squeezed her eyes shut to hold back tears—"Marty said you were God's gift, after the trial of Loretta. . . ."

I didn't want to hear this. "We should both get some sleep," I said, standing up. I drank my milk in one long gulp. "It'll be daylight soon."

Mama walked over and shut the back door, then drained her glass. "You never gave me any worry—oh, there was that trip to Mobile, but Sinclair says—"

"Come on, Mama. You're almost asleep on your feet."

"It's true," she said, and went first out of the kitchen. I turned off the light.

"Sweet dreams," she said.

forty-four

I did go back to sleep, but then morning came like a bee sting. My eyes were puffed up, and the light hurt; the shower water needled my skin. Uncle Marty was allergic to women, I thought. Now I'm allergic to myself. I've got this story that's going to poison me if I don't tell.

But Mama didn't want to hear. And I couldn't tell Mamby—she had her own pain to worry about. Deaton was too little and, besides, his tongue was loose at both ends. Keeping a secret was not his strength.

Loretta? Well, yes, if I could get her alone and make her stand still. Do it now, I thought. All we had to do before the funeral was get dressed and "pick up the house." (That's how Mama put it. I pictured us outside, lifting it by its four corners. . . .) Mamby wasn't coming till after we left for One-Way. She'd put out food for whoever gathered afterward. Usually they did this at the church, but Mama said she couldn't stand to be there without Uncle Marty, so we would have it at our house.

Loretta was usually up before daylight. She didn't come out right away, though, except to go to the bathroom. I don't know what she did in there. This morning I was pretty sure she'd had a shower before I did. Somebody had, or else I dreamed it. But I didn't remember any dreams after the one about the flood.

I got dressed and came out of the bathroom. Checked the kitchen, then listened outside Mama's room. Good. She was still asleep. I knocked softly on Retta's door. "Are you awake?" I asked.

"Is the Pope Catholic?" she asked.

"Can we talk?"

"Evidently."

"Loretta!"

"Just a minute, Sonny."

"I'll be on the porch," I told her.

It was one of those rare mornings in Alabama August when there was cool air coming from someplace. You could even smell it. The glider and porch chairs were damp, so I went back in and got a towel to dry them. Luckily the door hinges had all just been oiled; no give-away creaks. It's amazing what you do when someone dies.

I sat in the Tulip Chair, facing the glider and thinking how many times Uncle Marty had sat there with Mama, sipping sweet tea after supper. He wasn't allergic to her, because they loved the same person, a man who also used to sit in that glider with Mama. Or did he? Did we have the glider at the old house on Magnolia?

I asked Loretta this as soon as she came out. She was wearing a full red skirt and a skimpy white top that looked like one of Grandpa's undershirts with lace. Mama would never let her go to a funeral in that.

"You got me out here to talk about the *glider*?" Loretta said, plopping down on it.

"No," I said. "I just wondered."

"We had a different one on Magnolia," she said. "Dark green and white. But when they lifted it to put it on the truck, the swing hinges gave way. Rusted through. So they junked it."

"I see. I think I do remember that. It had a design on the back that felt like your skin when you have measles."

"God," Loretta said, looking out at the yard, not at me.

"You've got to help me," I said.

"With what?"

"If I don't tell somebody what happened with Uncle Marty I'm going to bust."

"Then spill," she said. "I've seen you pass out. I sure wouldn't want to see you bust."

"You won't tell anybody?"

"Who in this green hell would I tell?"

"Wesley."

"Sonny, Wesley hasn't got a brain to keep it in. Now go *on* before Selma gets up."

"Then why do you—" She looked daggers at me. "Okay," I said. "You know when I went to Mobile?"

"Yep. Summer Crisis Number One."

"It was because I found a letter from Daddy to Uncle Marty."

Loretta leaned forward. "You are kidding."

"No, I'm not. He wanted to know how we were and especially how I was doing in my job at the Circle of Life. Daddy knows all about us, Retta. He arranged for Uncle Marty to be his spy before he left."

"Holy cow!" Loretta said.

"Then the other day Deaton wanted to know what a queer was because Albion told him that the queers got Daddy. Remember that night when you and Wesley came home and we were sitting out here?"

She nodded.

"That's what we were talking about. Anyway, Deaton's question made me think about those men back in Mobile, those men who lived at the address on Daddy's envelope. And all of a sudden I knew that's what they were: queers. When I'd seen them, I sort of knew but I didn't know. So what did that mean? What was the connection with Uncle Marty? If he'd been in touch with Daddy, and he was really our friend, why didn't he tell Mama, who would give anything to hear from Daddy? Why was he keeping him to himself?"

"Slow down, Sonny," Loretta said. "You go too fast, you'll spin out on a curve."

I took a deep breath.

"Two more," she said.

I obliged, then plunged back in. "So two days before the fire I couldn't take it anymore. I told Uncle Marty I'd read Daddy's letter and been to Mobile and he had to tell me what was going on."

Loretta hit her forehead with the heel of her hand. "Jesus in a jukebox, Sonny! That was dumb!"

"Well, what would you have done?"

"I don't know, but not that. Go on."

"He got really mad—"

"Burned up, so to speak?"

"Retta!"

"Okay. Bad taste. I'm sorry."

"And he said to come back later after closing and we'd talk about it."

"And?"

I could feel my chest tighten, my throat start to close. I had to force the words out. "And when I did he said he'd loved Daddy since they were boys but Daddy didn't know it till he came to Uncle Marty and told him he'd—" My throat shut like a door.

"He'd what?" Loretta demanded.

I waved my hands, pointed to my neck.

"Day's wasting," she said.

"He'd gone to New Orleans," I said, in a squeaky little voice, "and fallen in love with a man."

"Go, Pops!" Loretta said. "So why was he confessing this to Uncle Marty?"

"Because he felt like he had to leave Mozier, and us, without a trace, and he wanted somebody to keep an eye on his family."

"His family he was deserting," Retta pointed out.

"Right. And when Uncle Marty heard this, he had to tell Daddy his feelings—"

"Throw *up*!" Loretta said.

"So that settled it. Daddy left the very next day."

Loretta covered her mouth and started laughing like crazy. "That *slays* me," she said.

I just looked at her. How could she take everything as a joke? I shook my head. She noticed.

"Well, what am I supposed to do?" she asked, her laughter evaporating. "You're telling me our disappeared daddy is a queer and our fake uncle, who just got incinerated in a donut shop, was his spy and I'm supposed to cry? Let me tell you something, Sonny. Life is a steam-roller. Take a situation like this—if you can *imagine* another situation like this—you take it seriously and it will crush you in no time flat."

"But what if you don't think it's funny?"

She leaned right in my face and whispered, "Change your *mind*."

"I'll try," I whispered back.

She smiled. "You'd better. It's a matter of . . . of laugh and death!" She hooted and slapped her thigh. "So then what happened?"

"I got really mad and I told him he was a spy and a liar and that according to One-Way, our daddy was going to Hell—"

"Uh-oh," Loretta said.

"And I knew I ought to quit right there but I was furious, so I said he wasn't in such a great light himself, and he said, 'Stop, please,' and I should have but I didn't. I went on to say the worst thing."

"Which was?" Loretta prompted.

"I said, 'Now that I know the truth, you expect me to keep quiet?'"

"Oh, Sonny." All the prance and sass went out of Loretta's voice. "You threatened him?"

I shivered. "Not exactly. I didn't say I *would* tell. But I brought up the possibility that I might."

"Expose him," Loretta added.

"Yes."

"Oh, brother," Loretta said, and she wasn't trying to be funny.

I hurried on. "But the next day I went back and told him I *wouldn't* tell, on account of how it would hurt Mama."

Loretta considered. "That's good," she said slowly. "Look, Sonny. The truth is not your fault. What you said wasn't great. In fact, that part about Leon and Hell, that was rotten. But the lies were Leon's and Uncle Marty's. You just made him look at some of the consequences. And you tried to do the same with our old man."

"'A beautiful man,' Uncle Marty called him."

"Yeah? Well, let him show some of that beauty around here with a hug or a birthday card or some reliable information about engines."

"I thought Wesley—"

"Sonny, you weren't listening! Wesley's brain, his total capacity for intellectual comprehension or synthesis or even rote memory, is the size of . . . of . . ." She reached over to the arm of the glider and picked up something between her thumb and forefinger. "Of this sow bug."

"So if you know that, why do you go out with him?"

"First off, he thinks I'm as beautiful as his Harley, and he knows I've got more gears. Second, he doesn't live in this house or belong to this family. And third, if he took a notion to leave me, he'd be too dumb to find the door."

forty-five

When we went in the kitchen we found Mama cleaning out the junk drawer. Stamp books, fly swats, extension cords, old bills, report cards, school pictures, and broken flashlights were strewn on the counter.

"Selma, have you flipped?" Loretta asked.

"This has been bothering me," Mama said, trying to unsnarl a tape measure caught on a barbecue fork. "*This* shouldn't be in here," she said, holding the wooden-handled two-tined tool as though it were a spear. "It could hurt somebody."

"You said we had to pick up the house, not dump it out," Loretta said.

Mama gave her a red-rimmed stare. "Have mercy," she said.

Loretta shut up.

Mama kept digging.

"I'm hungry," Deaton said. "I want pie."

"Help yourself," Mama said.

While she threw away old magazines and fishing line, bobbers and sinkers ("No!" Deaton protested; "They're broken," Mama explained), dried-out shoe polish, and Loretta's Brownie beanie, we ate pound cake, cherry pie, and Snow on the Mountain. And we all had coffee, Deaton putting so much sugar in his that the spoon only went halfway down. Finally Mama had two grocery bags for me to take to the trash, plus a bunch of stuff left sitting on the counter.

"What are you going to put in there?" Deaton asked, pointing to the empty drawer.

"Marty's things," Mama said. "Whatever he left us. I want them here where any of us can get them out when we need them. When we miss him most."

This was Loretta's cue to say, "*Miss* him?" in her super-sarcastic voice. Mama ignored her.

"What things?" Deaton asked.

"I don't know," Mama said, refilling her coffee cup. "They don't read the will till next week."

"I wish he left us the icing," Deaton said.

Mama sighed. "It was all lost."

"I know," Deaton said. "I just wish."

We stared at our plates. Everything felt strange, like the house was getting sick.

"I'll clean this up," Loretta said, taking her dishes and mine to the sink. Nobody told her to. I was thinking it must be habit from working at the Chat 'n' Chew when the doorbell rang.

"Run get it, Deaton," Mama said. She was in her robe.

Deaton ran down the hall, opened the door, and ran back. "It's a man," he said.

"Who?" Mama wanted to know.

"Somebody who said, 'Hello, Deaton.'"

I got up, and Loretta fell in right behind me. We went down the little hall and through the living room toward the man silhouetted against the sun.

There aren't any strangers in Mozier, I thought. Besides, he knew Deaton.

"I heard the news," he said. "I had to come home."

I searched his face. It was heavy, not angular the way I remembered. "It's not—," I started.

"I'm afraid it is," Loretta told me. Then she spoke to him. "Give me one reason why I should let you in."

"I'm your father," he said.

forty-six

Loretta didn't move. Deaton ran down the hall to the kitchen. I could hear his excited voice. "Mama! There's a man at the door who says he's Daddy!"

"That's pathetic," Loretta told the stranger.

Deaton shot right back down the hall. Mama, in her pink flowered bathrobe, came after him. She did not hurry. She stopped beside Loretta and looked up at the man, her left hand shading her eyes from the glare.

"Leon?" she said.

"I read about Marty," he said.

Now I saw he had a little suitcase with him.

"You heard about Marty?" Mama echoed. "And you're here?"

He nodded.

She started to laugh. At first it was just a giggle, like Jessie's and Jocelyn's after whispering something at the table, but then it turned into cascades, waterfalls of laughter. Tears poured down her face, and the weight of laughter began to bend her forward.

"Mama?" Was that concern in Loretta's voice?

"Selma—," Daddy said.

"Let him in!" Deaton demanded.

Like some reversible cloth, Mama's laughter flipped over into sobs. Loretta helped her to the couch. Huge gasps and moans came out of this little person, this quiet woman who was Mama. They sounded like they could pull everything out with them.

I caught Retta's eye. "Should we?"

"Oh, go on," she said. "Maybe he can fetch water."

I opened the door wide. Daddy walked in, looking around like he'd never been in a house before. He went over to the couch, to Mama, but he didn't touch her, didn't say anything. The sobs were quieter now, like a storm that's passed over and is moving on.

"I'm sorry," he said to Loretta. "I didn't—"

"Evidently not," she said.

"Do you have any brandy?" he asked. "It might help." He looked at Mama.

"There's the Get-Set bottle," Loretta said to me.

"I'll get it." I didn't want Daddy in Mama's bedroom.

Walking into the dim room, I saw that Mama's bed, the same pineapple four-poster she and Daddy had slept in, was already made up. On the dresser were pictures in dime-store frames: the three of us children in a swing at Grandma's; Grandpa in a boat holding up a big fish; and Uncle Marty in front of the Circle of Life. I'd never seen that one before. I lifted the Get-Set bottle from its place next to the china roses. It felt about half full.

When I got to the kitchen with it, Daddy was there. He'd gotten out a teacup but couldn't find a place to set it down.

"Mama took a notion to clean out the junk drawer," I told him.

"So I see," he said, then raised his eyebrows at the green-and-white plastic bottle I was carrying.

"Retta says Mama keeps gin in here," I said. I could still hear Mama, but it was just regular crying now.

"Let me see," he said, and I handed the bottle over. He took off its spray-pump top and sniffed the contents. "She could be right," he said, pouring a little in the teacup and tasting it. He made a face. "God! Selma could kill herself with this. It's gin, but it tastes like whatever came in the bottle. Is there any orange juice?"

I dug some out of the Frigidaire. He filled the teacup half and half and headed for the living room.

Loretta was sitting on the couch next to Mama, her

arm on Mama's bent-over back. Deaton was on the other side.

"If you'll move a minute, son—," Daddy said.

Deaton just glared at him.

"Give it to me," Loretta said, reaching out with her other hand. Daddy gave her the cup. "Come on, Mama," she said, as if she played Florence Nightingale every day. "Sit up and drink this."

Like a small child, Mama put both hands on the cup Loretta held and drank the gin and orange juice straight down.

"Thirsty," she said.

"In shock," Loretta added. Then she looked up at Daddy. "Just what the hell do you think you're doing, busting in on us like this?"

"May I sit down?"

"Yeah," she said. "But only because looking up at you hurts my neck."

He sat in Mertie's little wingback.

"I read about Martin's death," he said. "And I knew you all would be alone now."

"Spare me your kindness," Mama said, then hiccuped.

"Sonny had come looking for me," Daddy said in his defense. "He knew I was in touch with Martin."

"Sonny?" Mama looked up at me. I was the only one standing.

"That's why I went to Mobile," I explained.

"Lord help us, Sonny. Why didn't you tell me?"

"I didn't know how," I said, thinking, And you didn't want to know.

Daddy went on. "I even talked to him. *And* Deaton. Twice. On the phone."

"Well, la-dee-da!" Loretta said.

"So I've been in touch," he finished.

Mama gave out a hoarse sound, not a laugh or a sob, just something left over from both. She looked straight at Daddy, sitting in her dead sister's chair. "How long has it been, Leon? Seven years? Almost seven and a half? And you call two phone calls being in touch?"

It really *was* Daddy. I recognized him now, though he was older and thicker. His clothes were different, but they rested on his body in the neat easy way I remembered. His graying hair grew the same from that one spot on the back of his head, and his big hands were still slender, graceful.

"Selma, I *couldn't*," Daddy said, leaning forward in his chair. "And, you see, I had Martin. I asked him to watch over you."

"Watch over us?!" Mama exclaimed, and shot up off the couch.

"He described this house to me. He even sent pictures. And let me know—"

Mama lurched around the coffee table, grabbed Daddy

by the shoulders, and tried to shake him. But he was so big and she was so small, plus wobbly from grief and gin, she might as well have tried to shake a wall.

"You think we're"—she paused, out of breath—"some pack of dogs you can leave with the neighbors?"

Daddy got up. "No, Selma, honey. It was the only way I knew—"

"Don't you dare!" Mama said. She started to sway. He put a hand out to steady her. She jerked back.

"Martin Bonner was our friend, our deep friend in the Lord. And he *would* have been regardless of your . . . your cheap spying. So don't try to take that from me! You've taken more than you deserve all these years—" She looked around as she said this, as though acknowledging what was gone. "Don't think you can take Marty, too!"

And she walked out.

Cantaloupe walked in. She must have come in with Daddy and been hiding. She stood in the dining room doorway, her front legs straight out, then leaned back into a total stretch. When that was done, she walked over and started sniffing Daddy's shoes.

"Is that your cat?" Daddy asked Deaton.

"Don't touch her!" he said.

Daddy looked hurt. "You're a tough bunch," he said, and turned toward the door.

"See you at the funeral," Loretta told him.

forty-seven

We were all in our funeral clothes when Wesley came to pick Loretta up. Mama would have let her go, too, let her roar up to One-Way on a motorcycle with her dress flying, but Loretta said no, she needed to go with Mama. Wesley looked at her, lost.

"You can ride with us," she said.

"Can I drive?"

Mama shrugged. "If you have a license."

So it happened that we drove to One-Way with Wesley at the wheel, Loretta snug beside him, Mama riding shotgun, and me and Deaton in the back.

"Sinclair wanted to take us," Mama said as we rounded the corner onto Hawthorne. "But he rattles me sometimes, and I decided I didn't want any extra rattling today. Ha!"

"This Buick don't rattle at all," Wesley said.

Deaton looked at me.

"Mama," Loretta started. She'd apparently given up calling her "Selma," at least for this day. "What did you get out of Daddy besides us?"

I wanted to say, 'Cut it out, Retta,' afraid we were in for more tears, but Mama just looked at her daughter with something like respect. "That's a thoughtful question," she said.

Loretta let it rest.

When we got to the church, the gravel lot was packed with cars and the hearse was right up near the door. "'Hearse,'" Loretta declared, "was once an iron harrow with candleholders that they put over the coffin."

"No fooling!" Wesley exclaimed. "In Mozier?"

Loretta sighed. Our chauffeur pulled into one of the slots saved for family. He hadn't even cut the motor off when Mr. Wilt appeared in Mama's window.

"You can lean on me, Sister Bradshaw," he said. "I'll take you in."

Mama didn't hesitate. "Thank you, Mr. Wilt. But I've got Sonny."

Hearing that, I would have jumped out to open the door for her, but the Buick only had two doors. Mr. Wilt helped her from the car, his long thin arms spiderlike in his black suit. I climbed out behind her and offered her my arm the way I'd seen Uncle Marty do at Grandpa's service.

Remembering that made my eyes sting. He'd stood by us that day, had come "Yea, even unto the Methodists" to see Mama through her daddy's funeral.

Everybody was out of the car. Deaton held Mama's fingers, all he could get hold of because of the cast. Wesley and Loretta held hands, and we filed toward One-Way behind Mr. Wilt. As we got closer I could hear hammering, and I was thinking what an odd time to be doing repairs when Mr. Wilt stopped, pivoting on his heel to face Mama.

"We need to delay a moment, Sister Bradshaw," he said. "There's been a slight problem and I don't think it's corrected yet."

"What's that noise?" Mama demanded.

"There was a gentleman," Mr. Wilt began, his hands together with index fingers pointed like he was going to play "Here's the church, here's the steeple." He went on, "A gentleman from out of town who couldn't make it to the Visitation and requested to see the deceased—"

"Couldn't they get it open?" Wesley asked.

"Actually, that was not the problem. The problem is—"

"Lord God Almighty!" Mama said, pushing past him with her pocketbook and then using her cast to get by Uncle Sink at the door.

Bam! Wham! Bam! we heard as we practically ran into the Worship Room behind Mama. She strode up the aisle to the front, where the casket spray had been laid over the top of the upright piano and two men in dirty work clothes and tool belts were trying to get the silver coffin closed. Standing at the other end of the coffin was the "gentleman from out of town."

"Leon Bradshaw!" Mama exclaimed before she even got past the Slushers in row three. "Do you have to wreck funerals, too?"

Daddy looked like an orphan. "I wanted to say good-bye," he said.

"Are you satisfied?" Loretta hissed.

Bam! Wham! "Damn it!" one of the workers said, standing back and shaking his finger. There were little dents in the shiny surface now, though to the workers' credit whenever they were fixing to hit it they covered up that spot with a grimy towel.

Mama turned to Sister Clemons, who was at her post on the piano bench but could barely be seen for the flowers. "For God's sake, play something!"

"I can't see the notes," Sister Clemons said.

As if we'd practiced it, Deaton and I both walked over to the upright, which stood with its sounding board facing the faithful. This was so that when folks got the Spirit you could still hear the piano over the shouts.

Once we set the spray on the floor, Sister Clemons lit into "Are You Satisfied with Jesus?" and the hammering—the Anvil Chorus, Loretta called it later—went on.

"Damnedest thing I ever saw," one of the workmen said when they stopped for a minute so his partner could lean on the lid. "Fool thing just won't shut."

"Must be warped," the leaner said.

"He wasn't that fat," Wesley observed.

"If you weren't *so selfish*—," Mama said to Daddy. And the mourners sang:

> Yes, we're satisfied
> Lord, we're satisfied
> Yes, we're satisfied with You.

Suddenly Mr. Wilt spoke up. "I beg your pardon," he said, "but this lacks dignity." Loretta splurted out a laugh. "Could we—"

But before he could finish, Uncle Sink rushed down the aisle saying, "I'll fix it."

"You won't touch it!" Mama said. "I've seen your handiwork." Man, where was she when he was murdering my models? She turned to Mr. Wilt. "We'll put the casket spray back on and have the service and then see what you . . ." She looked at the coffin-closers, at a loss for the right word.

Loretta gave it to her. "Professionals," she said.

Mama nodded. "Professionals can do later."

So Deaton and I became flower-bearers again, with Mr. Wilt instructing us to place the spray just so, as if careful arrangement could rescue this memorial. The workmen disappeared out the side door, leaving tracks behind them and a hammer at Deaton's feet.

"Hand me that," Mama said, and Deaton did. She stepped over and presented it to Daddy. "Knock some sense into yourself," she told him, and then led us to the pew marked FAMILY.

We sat right up front, of course. And it was hot, hot, hot. All the windows had been propped open, but it was one of those afternoons when the air lay on top of you like a big cat, and no waving of cardboard Jesus-at-the-door fans could make it get up and move.

Grandma was there, along with the aunts and uncles and Albion, who was the last person I wanted to see, after Daddy. *You*, you started this, I wanted to say. You just like to slice people up with that razor tongue of yours and then laugh at them while they bleed. I had never beaten him up like I told Deaton I would. He was so tall and skinny he looked like you could push him over, but I knew better. I'd had those bony hands pin me to the ground, his green eyes flashing, while one knee pressed the breath out of me.

I *wanted* to think of Albion and not Daddy or Uncle Marty. I wanted to feel self-righteous. But it all boiled away when Sister Clemons lifted her fingers from the keys and Sister Dillard started singing from her seat:

Jesus paid it all,
All to Him I owe;
Sin had left a crimson pall,
He washed it white as snow.

I could picture Uncle Marty standing right where his unclosed coffin stood now, singing those words, his face twisted with feeling like a balled-up handkerchief.

A wave of voices joined Sister Dillard's, bearing her up, floating in the song like you float in a lake. "Paid it all!" someone called out, and "Thank you, Lord!" someone else answered.

All of a sudden everybody stood. Pastor Biggs had come to the podium. On the other side of Loretta, Grandma looked at her watch, then held up her wrist. We were starting twenty minutes late.

"Many waters cannot quench love," Pastor Biggs began, and Loretta pressed her thumb into my arm. I looked at her. "The fire," she mouthed, then took her thumb away, leaving a spot that would turn blue. She'd given up the red skirt and lace undershirt without a fight, and Mama had persuaded her to put on the kind of pale blue outfit that somebody sweet would wear. I don't know where it came from, but it made Loretta look like she had the wrong head. Beside her, Wesley leaned forward like a football player on the bench.

Pastor Biggs got through the Scripture and went on to how we were there to remember our faithful brother, Martin William Bonner. I was afraid to listen to this, so I started counting the roses—pink and white—on the casket spray Deaton and I had lugged around. I couldn't see it all, but I figured it had the same number of flowers on either side.

When I finished counting I thought about how they throw flowers in the sea when they slide sailors' bodies overboard and how in horse races, they blanket the winner with roses. I thought about the black-ribboned wreath of white roses on our door. Daddy had walked right past it.

So did he leave or was he sitting somewhere behind us? I wondered. Pastor Biggs had launched into a sermon about the loaves and fishes. He said Uncle Marty had fed the five thousand like Jesus did, only he'd used donuts and french fries and the Word of God. A faithful witness, he had served up the opportunity for salvation in every bite. Pastor Biggs described the menu board, which everyone knew about anyway, and said how I'd painted it. Then he said what a blessing Elder Bonner had been to our lives and what a blessing we had been to his. "Like his Lord, Martin Bonner ministered to the widows and the orphans, the outcasts, the deserted ones."

Out of the corner of my eye I saw the veil on Mama's hat tremble. Outcasts?

"And the Bradshaws gave him a personal family just as this church, this body of the Lord's faithful, gave him a family in the Spirit.

"Truly all things work for good in them that love the Lord."

Good? Uncle Marty was burned to death and Mama was deserted again and Pastor Biggs believed this was for the good?

No, he didn't. He was just saying that because he didn't have the guts to say the truth: that something stupid and horrible had happened and Uncle Marty's life was over. No words could touch that. He was gone. No words could be taken back, either. I'd said what I'd said, truth as far as I knew, and right or wrong I could never undo it. Never mind that now I knew Daddy wasn't worth looking for. Not because he was queer but because he had a heart the size of Wesley's brain. Where Marty's heart was big as the biggest dough bowl at the Circle of Life, big as that roaster Mama dropped the peeled peaches in the day Daddy left.

A bitter juice rushed into my mouth. Leon. We were

better off without him. Thanks to him they couldn't even close the coffin.

Tears spilled out of my eyes, and I didn't care. They weren't for Uncle Marty—those would come later—they were for the daddy that I had thought I had, the daddy I'd missed all these years, who I thought was off loving us perfectly somewhere, the daddy who never existed.

Loretta handed me some Kleenex she'd had the sense to bring though she never cries. Mama took hold of my hand. For the wrong reason, I thought. I'm not crying for who you think. But then I saw it didn't matter. Even Wesley was blowing his nose, and what did *he* have to cry about?

Pastor Biggs introduced the last song by saying, "Though Elder Bonner and the Circle of Life are gone from our midst, we know he's been welcomed into that greater feast in the Lord's house. Let us stand and sing number 131: 'Will the Circle Be Unbroken?'"

Loretta dug in her pocketbook for a pen, hunted for paper but couldn't find any, then wrote on the palm of her hand: TASTELESS. That got me through.

> I was standing by my window
> on a cold and rainy day
> when I saw the undertaker
> come to carry my father away.

> Well, I told that undertaker
> Undertaker, please go slow

MR. WILT, she wrote in the palm of her other hand.

> For the body you are taking
> Lord, I hate to see him go.

There was a wail from Mama and she stood up and flung her arms, cast and all, above her head, and the whole congregation rose to its feet like a flock of birds taking off. People started clapping to the music and Sister Goforth began shaking the tambourine. Amid moaning and foot-stomping, the song went on:

> Will the circle be unbroken
> by and by, Lord, by and by?
> There's a better home a-waiting
> in the sky, Lord, in the sky.

All around us people were shouting "Praise Jesus!" and "Gone to glory!" Finally the singing died down and the pallbearers went forward. They were struggling to lift the coffin when Mr. Wilt leapt up the aisle to remind them they couldn't carry it out because it still wasn't shut. On his way back he stopped at the end of our pew, signaling us to leave for the burial even if we didn't have anything ready to bury. He saw us to the door and started to turn back, but Mama latched onto his sleeve and pulled him outside.

She drew herself up to her full five foot three inches and let him have it. "I want to know what those men were doing hammering on that coffin. I don't know how you close them—"

"Sister Bradshaw," Mr. Wilt cut in, trying to stop her.

"—but I know better than to go at it with a hammer. That's no pine box they were whacking on. I paid for it, and I know."

"They *tried* to use the twirlies—," the undertaker began.

"The 'twirlies'?" Mama and Loretta said together.

"That's not the technical term," Mr. Wilt assured them.

"Well, yeah," Wesley said.

"In fact, it's a joke from *The Southern Planter*." Mr. Wilt was warming to his subject. He looked almost alive.

"'The Southern Planter'?" Loretta and Mama asked.

"They're like a Greek chorus," Grandma said, pleased with herself.

Mama swung her head around like she hadn't realized Grandma was there.

"Oh, that's not the real name," Mr. Wilt said with a

gargling sound that I guess is his version of a laugh. "It's our trade journal. It's really called—"

"I don't care if you call it 'Skulls and Shovels'—"

"All right!" Loretta said.

"—you get those people out of there and get your men in and do whatever it takes to—"

"Put a lid on it," Loretta finished.

Mr. Wilt threw up his hands at us and swung back through the door Elder Hudson was still holding open.

"There's a man don't know his own business," Wesley said. "I wouldn't want him undertaking on me."

"Me neither," Retta said. "I'd die first."

Just then Mama remembered that Grandma and Aunt Joy and all the rest of the relatives were standing there waiting.

"I don't know about you all," she said, "but I'm going to sit in my car till they bring Marty out. I can't be civil right now. I just can't."

So we sorted ourselves into vehicles and waited.

It was fifteen minutes before the Elders heaved the coffin into the hearse. Usually they carry it up the little hill to the cemetery. I was about to say this when Elder Slusher, panting a little, came over and leaned in the window across Wesley to tell Mama, "Don't you worry now. It's shut tight as a turtle's mouth."

Mr. Wilt got in the hearse and started the engine.

"Follow him," Mama commanded. "If Marty's too heavy to carry, I'm too hot to walk."

The graveside service didn't take long. Mama was too riled up to throw herself on the coffin like I'd been afraid she might. But she insisted on staying after everybody else had left.

"We'll take care of the interment," Mr. Wilt said, resting his bright white hand on the shoulder of her navy blue dress.

"I don't have utter confidence in that," Mama told him. "And anyway, I can't leave till you lay him in the ground. I've got this." She reached in her pocketbook and took out a paper sack like we take our school lunches in. She'd packed Uncle Marty a sandwich? "It's dirt," she explained. "From my yard."

"Is there no end?" Mr. Wilt asked, but Mama didn't seem to hear him. "Never mind. You and the children stand back," he said, as though it was his last breath. He directed the pallbearers to get on either side of the coffin, lift it by its big straps, hold it up so he could slide out the boards that kept it suspended over the grave, and then lower it slowly. It bumped the walls twice before settling. They pulled the straps out.

Deaton looked at me, a question in his eyes, but he didn't speak.

Mama opened the sack and said, "Each of you take some."

We did—even Wesley, who didn't understand that this was for family.

Mama led us up to the edge of the hole. Deaton peered in. Loretta held his collar.

"You take part of us with you," Mama said, then opened her hand and flung out the sandy dirt like it was flower seeds.

We all did the same.

"I'm sorry," I said, just to myself.

Then the two workers who'd struggled with the lid appeared behind Mr. Wilt, who stepped forward and put his hand on Mama's arm. "I'm afraid you have to go now, Sister Bradshaw," he told her. "The grave will be ready by five o'clock if you want to come back to visit."

Mama nodded. The men took hold of a tarpaulin covering a big mound of dirt off to the side of the grave, then peeled it back.

"Gol-lee!" Wesley exclaimed. "That's a right smart pile of dirt. Don't look like you could get all that dirt out of just this hole."

"They always look smaller from the top," one of the men told him.

And with that wisdom, we left Uncle Marty to rest in peace.

forty-eight

When we got home, Mamby had everything ready. Plates, silverware, and food were out on the dining room table, which was covered with the cloth she had washed and ironed. I went in the kitchen looking for her, but she wasn't there. Not in the bedrooms or the bathroom either.

I went out the back door and found her bent over, cutting flowers—the pink, purple, and white ones with ferny leaves and petals like little dishes. I couldn't remember their name. "Mamby," I said. "We're back."

She straightened up, flowers in her left hand, scissors in her right. "Your Uncle Marty loved cosmos," she said.

"Mamby," I said again, feeling all of a sudden like I might come apart.

And she gathered me into a hug just like I was Deaton.

"Daddy was here," I said when we separated.

"I know. He stopped in again on his way out of town. Left you something. I put it on your bed."

I ran up the back steps and into the kitchen, then turned around and held the screen door open for her. "Thanks, Mamby," I said as she came in.

Deaton was in our room, wearing nothing but his underwear and tie. "I can't get this off!" he said miserably, yanking the dark blue tie like it was a bell rope.

No wonder. I had tied it, and it wasn't right. It's hard enough to put one on yourself without having to do it backward on a seven-year-old.

"Hold still," I said, and worked the knot loose with my shaking fingers.

"Are you scared?" Deaton asked.

"No. Starved," I told him. We'd had dessert for breakfast and no lunch.

"Me too!" he said, and pulled on shorts and a shirt and ran out of the room. Somebody would send him back for shoes.

I looked on my bed. Nothing but Deaton's light blue suit coat, which had been Albion's and then mine before it was his. I picked it up, and there on the bed was a brown paper parcel.

"Expect nothing," I told myself, and opened it slowly. Wrapped in a dish towel I recognized—it had TUESDAY embroidered on it in green, and we still had SUNDAY in the kitchen—were three items: a yellow baby sock; a little metal Ford, its dark red paint about chipped off; and a white hair ribbon. I remembered Daddy "driving" that car over roads he made in my blanket or in the afghan on the back of the couch. It was just like the car he left in.

I found a note, too. The handwriting jolted me back to the day I read his letter at the Circle of Life. What if I'd never opened that drawer?

> Dear Sonny,
>
> You looked for me and then you didn't like what you found.
>
> I took these when I left so I would have something of my children with me.
>
> I'm sure they talk about forgiveness at One-Way. Try some. On everybody.
>
> Tell Loretta and Deaton I'm sorry that I couldn't stay.
>
> > Daddy

More stuff to bury, I thought. But not the note. I stuffed it all in my shirt drawer, picked up the rest of Deaton's clothes, and went out to join the family.

Already the house was filling up. The relatives had arrived, including Albion, whose head I wanted to pinch off but never would. Jessie and Jocelyn skipped through the dining room in dresses like upside-down roses. The Biggses, big and bigger, were in the living room with Mama, and assorted One-Way folks were talking on the front porch.

But one man wasn't talking, just leaning against the railing right where it was flecked with Retta's red fingernail polish. He looked familiar, but I couldn't—Ramey! Uncle Marty's deliveryman. I'd never seen him in anything but a jumpsuit. Surprising myself, I went out on the porch to welcome him.

"Too bad about Mr. Bonner," he said. "He was a good man. Honest. Friendly. And losing money hand over fist."

"He was in debt?"

"Oh, yeah."

My heart lurched. Uncle Marty had more secrets than I knew. "Did he owe you?"

"Owed the company, not me. I'm not hurting. Except I'll miss the old Scripture Mill."

I nodded. "Come in and have some dinner," I said.

Everybody was quiet, waiting for Pastor Biggs to pray. It was so hot with all those people in the little house that even the preacher kept it short. "Blessed Jesus," he said, "You fed the hungry, comforted the grieving, and raised the dead. Be with us now. Amen."

"Amen!" "Amen!" came from the couch and some-where near the china cabinet. Then Loretta called out, "Mama says to help yourselves."

They did. They fell upon that dining room table like boll weevils on a cotton field. And me starving.

I looked around for Deaton. He was sitting on the foot-stool in the living room with a full plate. I squeezed past three people to reach him. "How'd you get that?" I asked.

"Mamby fixed it for me," he said.

I headed for the kitchen.

Nissa was sitting at our table, big as life, cutting cake.

I stopped in my tracks.

She looked up and laughed. "Mama!" she said. "It's that boy that brought me Swiss steak."

I gulped and nodded.

"Looks like you could use some."

I nodded again. She was just so . . . beautiful. I saw her crutch propped against Mama's chair. I started count-ing the dessert plates on the table.

"So hungry you ate your tongue?" Nissa asked.

"No," I told her. "Just surprised." My voice sounded rusty.

Mamby was at the counter cranking an eggbeater. "I saved you a plate, Sonny," she said. "It's on the stove."

"Thank you," I said. And then one of Uncle Sink's say-ings popped out of my mouth. "I'm so hungry my stomach thinks my throat's been cut."

Nissa laughed again. It was delicious. I grabbed a fork, picked up the foil-covered plate, and took it to the table to sit with her. This time I'd be eating and she'd be watching.

"I know," Nissa said, just like I'd spoken out loud. "Looked like I was going to hole up in that house and turn to dust." She placed the tenth piece of cake on the tenth little plate. "But my daddy, he talked me into living." She glanced over at her mother, who at that moment turned around with a big bowl of whipped cream. "And Freelan's going to make it worthwhile."

"Thank the Lord," Mamby said, then looked at me. "This girl took a notion to get up and walk last night, and by this morning she was ready to meet the world. So I said she'd better make herself useful, and here she is."

"Freelan brought me," Nissa said.

I felt like a car wreck, but I ate. And it was good. When I was done, Mamby brought platters and bowls in from the dining room while I carried the desserts out. There was peach sauce as well as whipped cream for the pound cake. There was pie, too, and the cashew bars, but we had finished the Snow on the Mountain at breakfast.

"Sonny?" Mama called from the living room. I went over to her. "Where's your sister? She should be helping."

"I don't know," I said.

"Go look."

First I looked at Mama's plate. It was dotted with a spoonful of this and that, untouched. "You try to eat," I said.

Then I went down the hall and knocked on Loretta's door. No answer. I looked in. Empty.

I went out the back door and walked around the house. When I got to the front, I realized that Wesley's Harley was gone. I threaded through the eaters on the porch and went in to tell Mama.

"She picked a fine time to go for a joyride!" Mama said. "Mamby could use more help than just you."

"Nissa's helping," I told her.

"Well, praise the Lord," Mama said.

You get people in your house and give them food and it's hard to get them out. This crowd stayed till five-thirty and when they finally left even the furniture looked tired.

Mamby went through the rooms picking up the last of the glasses and coffee cups. Freelan had already come to get Nissa.

"You look ready for a rest," Mamby said to Mama.

"Past ready," Mama told her. "But I want to go back to the cemetery first." She got up from the chair where she'd sat all afternoon and carried her pie to the kitchen.

"Just leave the rest of this," she told Mamby. "We can take you home on our way."

"I'd like you to have a clean kitchen," Mamby said.

"That'll be Loretta's part," Mama replied. "She ought to do something."

So we went out to the Buick and its sizzling seats. Mamby started to get in the back but Mama said, "Let the boys ride back there."

We hadn't got off Rhubarb before Mamby, leaning toward the dashboard, said, "I've a mind to see his grave too. Could I go with you?"

Gol-lee! as Wesley would say. I knew in Mozier terms that was a lot to ask.

Mama breathed it in and studied on it while hand over hand she turned the wheel that hauled us around the corner.

"Of course," she said.

Mamby leaned back.

One-Way looked deserted when we pulled in the drive. That was good. But when we got up close I saw Wesley's motorcycle.

"Help my time!" Mama said as she cut the engine off. "What are they doing here?"

We soon found out.

Before we got to the grave we could see that the flower arrangements were laid around it, not on top the way you'd expect. But only when we got right up to it could we tell why.

Every inch of that fresh-piled Alabama dirt was covered with donuts. All kinds, laid edge to edge, making a chocolate and maple, cinnamon and plain-glazed coverlet, making a Circle of Life quilt. Donut boxes were stacked where the tombstone would be and Loretta had written on them with a grease pencil, sharing the message among the boxes: O TASTE   AND SEE   THAT THE LORD   IS GOOD.

I held my breath.

Mama burst into tears. "It's perfect," she said, and opened her arms to Loretta.

Deaton pulled on Mamby's sleeve. "Are those to eat?" he asked.

"No, child," she said. He looked crushed, but she was smiling.

"It was Wesley's *idea*," Loretta said over Mama's shoulder. He beamed.

Anything could happen.

Part Three

1956

forty-nine

Anything could happen—and some of it did. But not right away. I started high school and Loretta became an almighty senior. Nell and I walked to school together, went to ball games, held hands. By Christmas I was hovering around being in love. I wanted to go steady, but Nell said we should just *be* steady, and we are. I like that.

Loretta and Wesley, on the other hand, are kaput. Wesley gave her a diamond ring for graduation, and she put it right on and wore it for two and a half months. Then at the end of the summer she gave it back and broke his heart. She said it just dawned on her that he was not a pillar holding up her life but a tree fallen across her road.

For three August nights Wesley stood and howled on the sidewalk across the street from our house. "Sounds like a just-weaned calf," Grandma said. Loretta didn't say anything. She was packing. She had decided to go up to the university.

At first Mama said, "Oh no, you don't!" because of the trouble at Tuscaloosa last fall. A colored girl had enrolled in school and folks had gone wild. There were pickets and soldiers and speeches from the governor and the president. But Loretta said, "If I can't go to Birmingham, I'll go somewhere worse like New York." And Mama knew she meant it.

"I hope Birmingham is ready," Mama told Loretta. But she was half smiling. That donut blanket on Marty's grave had changed things between them.

And it wasn't just Mama accepting Loretta. Or Loretta suddenly seeing Mama. It was them becoming more alike. For instance, around Halloween after Marty died Mama decided to tell the truth about Daddy. First she told us kids, as if we didn't already know—well, Deaton didn't, of course, and he blurted out, "Albion told me that a long time ago, but Sonny swore it was a lie!"

"I thought it *was* a lie then," I said.

"'Then'?" Mama's voice went up.

"I mean, now I know. You just told me." I didn't sign up for truth-telling.

Once she had us informed, she told Grandma and her sisters. She did this in the kitchen when they were cleaning up after a Sunday dinner. I heard the first line as I came out of the bathroom, and I stayed in the hall to listen to the rest.

Somebody had just cut the water off when Mama said, "Have you ever just all of a sudden known something that you didn't know you knew?"

"Well, of course," Grandma replied.

"I usually don't like it," Aunt Roo said.

"Maybe Mama should sit down." That was Aunt Joy, talking about Grandma. A chair was scooted out, then scooted back in heavier.

"Am I going to want to know this?" Grandma asked.

"Probably not," Mama told her.

"Then why—?" Aunt Roo started.

"It's important to me," Mama said.

I could picture Aunt Roo rolling her eyes. Then somebody turned the water on full blast. That was probably her too, trying to drown Mama out.

"Shut that off," Grandma ordered. "And you all sit down. You're making me nervous."

"See?" Aunt Roo challenged.

Water off. More chairs scooting.

"When Leon was here, you know, for Marty's funeral—"

"Lord, Lord," Aunt Joy murmured.

"I looked at him—and I swear I saw this from his suit jacket, the way *it* came near me but *he* didn't—and I realized, and Roo you may have tried to tell me this—"

"Not me!"

"—only I hadn't wanted to know, all those years ago when Leon left, and before. After all, we had three children, bone of our bone, and surely they were proof that it couldn't be . . ."

Aunt Joy took advantage of this pause. "Selma, honey, just say it."

". . . That Leon was, that our marriage wasn't real because he was . . ."

Mama got right up to the word but nothing came out. Silence.

Then somebody stood up so fast they knocked something off the table. Whatever it was, it didn't break, just rolled.

"You don't mean to tell me"—this was Grandma's voice, and it had more steam behind it than I'd heard since Grandpa died, "that Leon Bradshaw is a *Homo sapien*!"

Aunt Roo laughed but tried to hide it in a cough. Aunt Joy exclaimed, "Lord have mercy!"

And Mama said slowly, like she'd practiced, "*Sexual*, Mama. It's homo*sexual*. And yes, that's exactly what I mean to say."

Oh, man! I had to get outside before I choked. And I had to find Loretta. This was just too good.

fifty

Before Loretta left, we took a walk and wound up down on Hawthorne right where the Circle of Life used to be. It's a gas station now. We stood in silence for a minute by the Free Air hose and then Loretta said, "Now they're pumping gas where Marty used to serve up the Gospel."

I nodded.

"You got to let it go, Sonny," she said.

"Oh, I have, I have."

"Like hell you have. You haven't eaten donuts in a year."

"The ones from Piggly Wiggly are stale," I said.

"You haven't drawn either."

"I never was any good."

"You *liked* it," Loretta stressed. "And Marty thought you were God's gift to graphite."

"Well, Marty's—"

"My point exactly. But you don't have to bury stuff with him."

"Did I say I did?"

"Sonny, you were a kid. Marty was a man. You had every right to look for Daddy and try to get answers when you couldn't find him. What that set off in Marty was his own stuff. If—and this is a big *if*—he did 'commit sideways' as the visionary at the funeral home put it, he tied the wet shoelaces around his own neck. Not you, Sonny Boy."

This made me mad. "So I'm your project now that you've dumped Wesley?"

"No. It's just that since I've stomped on his heart, you're the only man I can count on."

"That's pathetic," I told her.

"Our whole *life* is pathetic," she pointed out. "Mama taking up with Mr. Fritch and his wife barely unpacked in the next world. Deaton breaking Albion's jaw—"

"*That* I liked."

"But over a hot dog?"

"It wasn't that and you know it."

"Yeah, but nobody else did," Loretta said. "He could get kicked off the Sluggers for assaulting a fan."

"Albion shouldn't have stayed here. He's got too much history."

"He has to be here to hate Uncle Sink," she said. "It's his mission."

We started walking again.

"I'll write to you," I said.

"Don't."

"Why not?"

"I won't read it," she declared. "If you want to communicate with me, you've got to draw."

"Oh, Loretta!"

"I'm serious."

"Will you draw back?"

She laughed. "*I'm* not an artist. It would be a drawback if *I* drew back."

I didn't smile.

"Okay. Once. If you draw to me, I'll draw back once."

"A deal," I said.

The first letter I sent was two images: the Buick's steering wheel with the dashboard behind it—because I was finally learning to drive, spells or no spells—and Loretta's stripped-down room. Gone were her Elvis poster and her motorcycle engine diagram and her lipsticks lined up in double rows like pistons.

What she drew back was a stone arch with open gates that I guess was supposed to be the entrance to the university. A little sign posted on one pillar said:

ITCHING TO LEARN?

TRY THE POISON IVY LEAGUE.

In reply, I started to draw our doorway with the three-leaved threat climbing around it like roses. I was going to put a sign on the mailbox that said, EDUCATION STARTS FROM SCRATCH, but before I got the vine halfway up the doorpost, I went cold all over and then hot and would have thought I was getting sick but I was MAD, too, like when you say "MAD AS FIRE," so I wadded up the paper and rushed out of the house. I didn't think where I was going but just followed the creek to the river.

I still had the crushed drawing in my hand.

When I got to the edge I pitched the paper like some weightless baseball. It landed on the dark green water and floated away. "Many waters cannot quench love" swam into my head. "Many waters . . ." And then I knew why I'd run from that drawing. It was like the menu board! It was "I am the vine and ye are the branches" all over again, only this time the vine was poison. My throat hurt like somebody had stepped on it.

"Marty!" I yelled. It was a ragged sound. And there was nobody to hear, just the weeds and the river. "Daddy!" Long gone.

I stood there awhile, breathing hard. Gradually I cooled down. But I was too agitated to go back to the house, so I went for a walk on the riverbank. After about a mile I came around a bend, and who should I see but

278

Nissa and Freelan and their baby, Billy, sharing a picnic on a quilt.

Nissa looked up. "My Lord, Freelan, it's that Bradshaw boy sure as I'm living!"

"Hi, Nissa," I said. "Hi, Freelan."

"Billy, too," she insisted.

"Hi, Billy," I said. "How are you all?"

"Starving," said Freelan. I could tell he meant *Scram!*

"You want a chicken wing, Sonny?" Nissa asked.

"No thanks," I said. "I've got to get home."

"Not in this direction you won't," Freelan said, and gave me a look. I remembered Mamby saying that he'd lost all patience with white folks.

"That's true," I said, and set my foot in the other direction.

Billy started to whimper and Nissa bit the loose parts off a drumstick bone and gave it to him to chew on. "He's cutting teeth," she explained.

I nodded. She was still beautiful, only rounder. Not a girl anymore.

Nissa went on, "Come March, he'll be a brother."

"Oh," I said, backing away from them in my mind. "Congratulations!"

"So we survived our losses, huh, Sonny?" she said.

"Nissa," Freelan said, like he was saying *Stop.*

I didn't know how to answer her.

"You had your runaway daddy and I lost my leg."

"Yes," I said, amazed that she remembered that talk.

"And then there was that burned-up donut man."

"Yes, ma'am," I said, feeling unreal.

Nissa laughed. "I'm no 'ma'am' to you, Sonny. I could be your sister."

"Nissa!" Freelan said. He hissed it like a warning.

"Simmer down," she told him, laughter still shiny in her voice. And then to me, "It don't do to be stuck. Have some chicken," she said again.

"Okay," I told her.

And she handed me a crisp, golden wing.

fifty-one

I thought about Mamby drinking coffee with Mama the day after Marty died, about her coming with us to his grave. And I sat down on the blanket, Freelan or no Freelan.

"What are you up to?" Nissa asked, deftly using her napkin to wipe drumstick drool off Billy's chin.

"I'm learning to drive," I said.

"Good," she said. "You'll go places."

"All white boys go places," Freelan said, disgusted.

"Oh, hush," Nissa said. "This is Sonny I'm talking to."

"I wish you wouldn't."

"Then you're wasting wishes," Nissa told him.

I started to get up.

"Whoa there," Nissa said. "Don't let him run you off."

Anger hardened Freelan's face. He stood up, turned, and walked away.

Nissa shrugged her shoulders. "So where you gonna drive to?" she asked.

"I don't know," I said. "Just around Mozier for a while. It's not like I have a car. But sometime I'd like to go up to Birmingham to see Loretta or maybe back to Mobile."

"To find that no-good daddy?"

"No," I said, but I smiled. This surprised me so much that I smiled some more.

"Want a biscuit with some of these fried apples on it?"

"Sure."

She spooned the apples in and handed me the biscuit on a flowered napkin.

Billy was done gumming the drumstick and started hitting the blanket with it. His force was greater than his balance, and he fell over.

"Whoopsie!" Nissa said, setting him back up. He looked startled, like it was the world that had gone sideways and then come back, not him.

"What are *you* up to?" I asked.

"Mostly this baby and that man," she said.

"That seems like plenty," I said, and took a bite of the apple biscuit.

"We still got room for a girl," she said, patting her belly. "Freelan's a peck more trouble than babies."

"I'm sorry," I said.

She laughed. "Oh, stop being sorry!" she said. "You been sorry since the first time I laid eyes on you."

"That's because you were in the hospital," I said.

"I was," she said, "but you brought that sorry in with you."

I didn't know what to say.

"Didn't you?"

"I don't know."

"Well, I do. You had the miseries over your disappeared daddy."

I nodded.

"Then you had the miseries over me."

I felt the blood rush to my face. And elsewhere.

"And then that fat old donut man—"

"He wasn't old," I protested.

"But there's always something, isn't there, Sonny? Something to be sorry for."

Billy, waving the drumstick, poked himself in the eye and wailed. Nissa scooped him onto her lap.

"I guess," I said.

"Well, you're right," she said. "There is. But there's usually something to laugh at too, something to float your heart on the river of life like a bobber instead of a sinker. You got to look for that."

I nodded.

"You take Freelan," she went on.

"No thanks," I said.

Nissa laughed. "You two are a lot alike."

"Wait a minute!"

"No, listen. Freelan used to be a laughing man, but now he carries *injustice* around the way you carry *sorry.*"

Shoot. I sure didn't want to be on any list with Freelan.

"But there *is* injustice," I said.

"'Course there is. And there's always stuff taken from you, like your leg or your daddy or your rights. And you got to fight to get back what you can. But there's also biscuits, Sonny. And babies." Hers was rubbing his face against her breasts. "This one's getting sleepy," she said, and kissed him on the head.

"Freelan wants to make things better," I said. "He wants what's right."

"Sure he does," she said. "And I love him for that. I love him for standing up and saying things has got to change."

"So what's the problem?" I asked, aware all of a sudden that, in spite of myself, I had wound up on Freelan's side.

"The problem is, if you're gonna be mad till the world is perfect, you're going to be mad the rest of your life. If *sorry* is the baby you carry everywhere with you, there's no room in your lap for joy. It can't all be struggle—that's what I tell Freelan. You miss the biscuits, you miss the babies," she said. "You miss what's right in front of you."

"You're amazing," I said.

"Mama raised me right," she said.

"She partly raised me, too."

"That's it!" Nissa said with so much energy that Billy jumped. "I'll tell Freelan that you're just about his brother-in-law."

"Please don't," I said, and we laughed.

"You go on now," she said. "I think Billy and me will just take us a little nap."

"But—"

"You go on. Freelan'll be back in a while."

"Okay," I said, getting to my feet.

"Don't be sorry," she said.

"Don't you worry."

"I don't," she said, laughing. "Don't *you* worry."

"Bye, Nissa."

"Billy, too," she said.

"Billy, too."

fifty-two

I'd forgotten till I got home and found Mamby down on her knees in the living room trying to get the wand of the sweeper under the couch that the whole family was coming to supper. It was Sunday, but with Loretta gone, Mama had asked Mamby to come and help her get ready. I don't know why Mama makes such a big deal of things. We could have had baked beans and wieners. I know how to fix those.

But no. Mama was in the kitchen wrapping chicken around ham wrapped around cheese and Mamby was cleaning house.

Someday, when I have a house, it won't even have furniture. The heavy stuff, I mean. It'll have a bed, a card table, a folding chair or two, and a television. That's it. The one bad thing about Loretta breaking up with Wesley is that his family has TV and sometimes I got invited over to watch it. So I want one of those. And I want all my stuff to be new. It won't cost a lot—except the TV—because I won't have much, and anyway it will be worth what it costs not to have dead relatives whispering every time you sit down in a chair.

"Where's Deaton?" I asked after I'd got through Mama's ten-minute explanation of what she was doing to the chicken.

"Gone door-to-door to feed the hungry," she said, tucking each piece of Chicken Cordon Bleu into a pan like she used to tuck Deaton into his crib.

"He could bring them over here," I offered.

"It's Scouts," she said. "And you are not funny."

"I am not Loretta," I said, which surprised me. Then, though I had hoped to escape to my room as soon as I'd let Mama know I was home, I heard myself asking, "Is there anything I can do?"

"Help Mamby put in the table leaves," she said.

"Where are they?" They had just appeared on the day of Marty's funeral. Usually when the family came over Mama set the food on the dining room table, we filled our plates, and ate on our laps.

"Under my bed," she said. She was bent over putting the chicken in the Frigidaire. "Lift them out, Sonny. Don't drag them. I don't want them scratched."

So I went in the bedroom, which had some sort of flower smell. Not roses. The purple ones that bloom in the spring. Lilacs. Anyway, like Mamby I got down on my knees and lifted first one leaf out and stood it against the wall, and then went back for the other. Just then the telephone rang. I went to the hall to answer it. The sweeper was still roaring.

"Hello!" I said as loud as I could without yelling.

"Sonny?" a man's voice asked.

"Yes!" I pressed my voice into the phone. "Who's calling?"

"Your daddy," he said. Something in my chest caved in. "How are you?"

I took a deep breath, pushing my chest back out. "I'm fine. But Mamby's sweeping and I can barely hear you. Do you want to talk to Mama?"

"Yes. But unplug that thing first!"

"Hold on."

I put the receiver crosswise on the phone cradle and went to the kitchen. Mama was slicing olives and sticking them on little rafts of celery stuffed with pimento cheese.

"Telephone," I said. And then, to be fair as she started for the hall, wiping her hands on her apron, I added, "It's Daddy."

"Surely not!" Mama said, which was not what I expected. "Would you get Mamby to turn off the sweeper? And see if she needs help."

In the living room, the sweeper was running but Mamby was looking out the window.

"Mamby," I said, and she turned around slowly, then shut off the Electrolux with her foot. I just stood there, aware that because I'd interrupted her, I'd seen her real face for a second—tired and worried and a little impatient—before her working-for-white-folks face took over again.

"What is it, Sonny?"

"Daddy's on the phone," I said. "Mama's talking to him. She says you might need some help."

"Good," Mamby said. "Help me move this couch then, Sonny. I'm a little down in my back."

She took one side and I took the other, and though I tried to hear the hallway conversation, it was impossible over the noise we made. Mama was talking really soft. We lifted and scooted and Mamby bent over what looked like a dirty sock. "I thought so," she said, standing up with something white curled in her palm. It *was* a sock, but there was something on it. A kitten.

"It's dead?"

She nodded. "Born too soon, looks like. Hand me that dust rag," she said, pointing to the end table. It was a piece of my old blue sweatshirt. "It's clean." She wrapped the kitten up and gave it to me. "Put it in a sack and put it up somewhere. Your brother will want to bury it when he gets home."

"You sure know Deaton," I said. And I wondered again what it was like for Mamby to have these kids who were not her kids and keep this house that wasn't—

"Always been like that," Mamby said.

Once the table was set, the bathroom shining, and the potatoes boiling, Mama sent Mamby home. Then she said I should get cleaned up.

"I will," I said. "But what did Daddy want?"

"To talk to me," she said.

"Why now?"

"I don't know, Sonny, except—" The doorbell rang. "That's them!" she said. "I'll get it. You change your shirt."

"But Mama—," I started.

"Go on. We'll talk later."

By six o'clock we were all seated around the table: Mama, Grandma, Uncle Sink and Aunt Joy, Aunt Roo and Uncle Hickman, Jessie, Jocelyn, Deaton, and me. Grandma and the aunts exclaimed over the fancy chicken but Uncle Sink said, "Give me plain old fried chicken any day."

Mama ignored him and began to explain how she fixed it.

"First you pound the chicken breasts with a meat hammer—"

Uncle Sink laughed. "Just like a woman," he said.

"Couldn't hit a nail to save her soul but she still wants in on the hammering."

Mama stood up and said, "Stop it, Sinclair."

Uncle Sink laughed harder. "It's the truth," he said.

"I am tired of being ridiculed," Mama said, and walked around the table and took his plate.

"Whoa, Sis—," he protested.

"I'll give it back when you apologize," she demanded.

"What for?"

"Just say you're sorry, Sink," Aunt Joy advised.

"But I'm *not* sorry," he said. "I'm accurate. Why, I knew a woman once who thought she could be a plumber—"

"Then you're not welcome at my table," Mama cut in.

"Selma," Grandma said, "He's your *brother.*"

"And he ought to treat me with respect," Mama said.

"Your upsetting Mama," Aunt Roo cautioned.

"*He's* upsetting *me*!" Mama said.

Then Uncle Sink stood up.

"Sinclair," Aunt Joy said, both a plea and a warning in her voice.

He glared at Mama, his face rusty red. "I'm going," he said. "But listen here, Selma Estelle. Don't you call me when your water's cut off or your sewer backs up or your boy over there"—he jerked his head at me—"has a fit."

"Don't worry," Mama answered. "I won't.'

Then he stomped off through the kitchen and slammed the back door and was gone.

"Aren't you going home with your husband?" Grandma asked.

Aunt Joy gave a deep sigh.

"Well, I never," Grandma said.

"Are you all right, Mama?" Aunt Roo asked. All eyes turned to Grandma.

"Of course she's all right," Mama said. "She's not made of feathers."

That settled things down. We finished the chicken—which was good, actually—and shelley beans, the slaw and broccoli and light rolls. Folks even talked again once Mama served coffee and ribbon cake, the recipe for which she also explained. It involved sherbet, the freezer, and "a little coping saw."

"By the way, Sonny," she said when she'd given all the details, "what's in that lunch sack in the freezer?" That's where I'd put the kitten. I'd written my name on it.

"Oh, nothing," I said.

Mama lowered her head and looked at me over the dime-store glasses she wears now.

"I mean, I'll tell you later."

"Sonny—," she insisted.

Deaton had come in at the last minute, so I hadn't had a chance to tell him yet, but this was not the night to cross Mama.

"Cantaloupe had a kitten under the couch," I said. "It was dead and Mamby and I found it."

"Oooh! Gross!" said Jessie.

Deaton jumped up and headed for the kitchen.

"Come back here," Mama said. "It will keep. That is, I believe, the purpose of the freezer."

I could feel a wavery moment where Deaton almost didn't turn around. But he did. He wasn't a little boy anymore.

He sat down.

"This cake was in the freezer?" Grandma asked.

"It was," Mama said.

Grandma put down her fork. "With a dead cat."

"It's just a kitten," I told her. "Pretty dried up. And wrapped in a dust rag—"

"Saints preserve us," Aunt Roo said.

"—and I put *that* in—"

"Enough, Sonny," Mama said.

"That's enough for me, too," Grandma said, folding her napkin carefully and laying it beside her plate.

"More coffee?" Mama asked, but suddenly everybody was scooting back their chairs and standing up and getting ready to go home. And though the aunts cleared the table like always, they didn't stay to help with the dishes.

After they had gone and Deaton had taken the kitten out to the backyard to bury it, Mama sat down at the kitchen table with a second cup of coffee. I don't like the stuff but I poured some too, then sat down. A grown-up move.

"So why did he call?" I asked her.

"It's our anniversary," she said.

"I didn't know that!"

"Well, why would you? It hasn't been celebrated in living memory."

"But what made him call this year?"

"He wanted to tell me something," she said, and she didn't look mad. In fact, she looked hopeful. Not about him, though. Not like she looked all those years ago when every check he sent made her think he might be coming back.

What did he say? I wanted to ask. It must have been something pretty big. . . . Then I had a thought. "Was that why you stood up to Uncle Sink?"

"Leon's call?" She put down her cup and raised her eyebrows at me.

Now you've done it! I said to myself.

But Mama shrugged her shoulders. "Oh, maybe," she said. "But I'd about had it with Sink anyway. He's such a . . . such a . . ."

"Drain," I said. And we both laughed.

"I miss Loretta," Mama said.

"Me too."

"All those years I thought she'd be the death of me, and I miss her."

Just then Deaton came in the back door. He had a cardboard box with TIDE printed on it.

"I'm putting this in our closet," he said. "For the *next* kittens."

"You do that," Mama said.

So much for talking about Daddy's call.

"Okay if I go over to Nell's?"

Mama sighed. "Be sure you're home by ten," she said. "You've got school tomorrow."

fifty-three

I'd never told Nell what happened with Marty, never told anyone except Loretta, but that night I felt like the time had come.

We sat on her porch steps. The story was long and we got cold but Nell didn't complain. She put her hand in mine inside my jacket pocket and just listened, saying "Oh" and "Um-hmm" every once in a while to keep me going. When I got to the night of Marty's death she squeezed my hand, so close, like she was a part of me.

"Grown-ups sure make a mess," Nell said.

"You can say that again."

"I'm sorry you had to get caught in it. It's not fair."

"Thanks."

"What made you tell me now?" she asked.

"Well, I was getting to that," I said, and launched into the tale of the company and the phone call and the dead kitten. I finished by saying, "And Mama won't tell me a thing he said!"

"I should hope not," she said.

Just then somebody flicked the porch light off and on twice.

"That's the 'Stop kissing' signal," Nell explained.

"But we weren't kissing!"

"Well then," she said, and leaned toward me till our lips touched. Her mouth was warm and soft and sweet. When she sat back, she said, "I guess it was the 'Start kissing' signal."

"I love you," I said, reaching over to ruffle her hair.

"I love you too," she said. "And that's what matters. Not old love gone bad."

"You mean Daddy calling?"

"I mean all of it. The call. Marty. Your mama. And my mother and father and their fights—that's *their* story."

"But I'm part of my parents' story," I insisted. "It's my childhood."

Nell freed her hand and turned to face me. "In your childhood you were part of their story. Now it's time for your own."

"Oh," I said. And suddenly it wasn't just my feet and face that were cold. I felt cold inside my chest, too. Bleak.

Empty. "But what am I without them?" I asked Nell.

"That's what you have to find out."

I took a deep breath. "You'll help me?"

"I'll be with you," she said.

"I'll remember that," I said.

"Good."

It *was* good. She was good. I was good. "Right now I'm the guy who's going to kiss you again," I said.